1

WE'D BEEN TRUNDLING over the moors for some time, where mysteries seemed to lurk amidst the tangled heather, silent pine plantations, dark cliffs that watched forlorn upon the lonely lane we wandered, and the time that bound us all together. And with the perfume of the pine and the babbling of the streams that trickled by, we could be reassured that most of our senses were working and knew still how to function as a source of satisfaction.

As we moved, the worn-out drystone walls, perhaps no longer knowing much function other than a fitting addition to the ambiance and aesthetics of the place, were becoming more numerous, while heather turned to rugged grass stretched bare across the lower land, and this new harmony let gentle fields come sidle idly by. The odd cliff continued though, as forlorn as ever, and so did the uneven ground, which gave way to fields of better character than those you might naturally imagine, particularly if you were imagining an arable land in a southern place. Stubborn twisted trees also persisted, sometimes in clusters and sometimes just alone, battling on and unbroken by lack of company. And these ones drew the eye, or perhaps the soul, for they made the world seem wilder, and all the more worth wandering. With the odd wood-smoked sleepy village, adorned by an old pub to welcome the weary and a lone telephone box that was red, sitting nestled between all this that nature had offered, everything crescendoed to give a feeling of goodness while indeed accompanied by a familiar undertone of sorrow, that seems to represent what life is, or inescapably must be, at its finest.

"This is an old Roman road." the coachman called out abruptly.

A short pause ensued as my companion and I exchanged a glance and measured who was best qualified to respond to this with acceptable quality.

"OK…" I said, feeling the pause had become long enough.

I worried it was suboptimal, we both did perhaps, but it was too late, the chance to pretend we hadn't heard the driver's commentary was long gone. After a few minutes of continued tension, my companion rallied to try and break it.

"I thought Roman roads were straight," he said, "this road doesn't seem very straight."

Good point, I thought, *good point*. We looked in excited anticipation to the driver's response, knowing that we might

PALE PIECES

Pale

Pieces

G.M. STEVENS

Pale Pieces

First Edition 2025

ISBN 978-2-9596757-0-6

www.gmstevens.com

But to what purpose, disturbing the dust on a bowl of rose-leaves, I do not know.

— T. S. Eliot

have found fault in something someone had said, but moments passed, and none came. I think he'd pretended not to hear us.

So we passed on a while in silent reflection, each considering our little bit of world in our own respective ways, until silent reflection must have met the limits of its comfort.

"Look at all those sheep," my companion said, motioning out across the passing fields, "lying down — they must be sleeping."

I'd been looking at them myself, these dull white shadows now, glowing silently through the dim. You could see them over the stone wall (*actually maybe function still remained*, I thought), almost completely still and silent, perhaps bowing now to the law of bedtime, as we all must, even when excited and raring to stray, lest we regret late night flippancies the following day. It was almost like a dream as we trundled creakily through and past this other world of silent glows, and we were perhaps reminded that, even when worlds apart, we were all in this world together — worn-out walls, the sheep, nightly things that creep, dark lanes, creaking wheels, and we.

"Are they lying down?" I decided to reply, "I think they're still standing up, albeit quietly…"

"They're not making a sound and they're not even moving!" my companion scoffed as we peered through the mirk, "They must be asleep!"

"Yeah, what if sheep sleep standing up?" I proposed, "Is that possible? Maybe sheep can sleep standing up…"

I was a bit hesitant to suggest this, as it risked mockery,

and not just now I thought, but as a sort of long-term anecdote that might be recited for mild amusement at dinner parties and things like that, which made it even more risky.

"Uuhhh?" he replied, looking confused.

I deemed he wasn't sure if I was joking or not and so could only emit sound that's born from a conflict of thought, so this worked out well.

"I've sheen seep shleep standing up loads of times." the driver called back to us.

"What really?" I said, too excited perhaps to mock his slip of tongue, even internally, which should have really been obligatory.

He chuckled back as he gave his reins a whip, and that was annoying because I wasn't sure whether he was joking or not — maybe he was just amused at his own slip of tongue for example. I looked over at my companion, and he was looking at me. So caught up in a web of confusion/social tension which seemed to be of our own making, we just sighed a bit and let the carriage push on, through the dull white silent glows. But finally it was nice, because even where sheep are concerned, it seems there still lie mysteries that guard the magic of the world, which already wanes so with the weight of apparently organised data.

"You know, I don't wanna know," the driver piped up again, "I like to trundle past, and wonder."

"You don't want to know what?" we said in unison.

But no response came.

"…What doesn't he wanna know?" my companion murmured over, looking pleadingly at me. But I just had to look back blankly, feeling a state of surrender coming on.

Our journey on the little coach that had braved wild moors, impending nightfall, and sustained converse under social strain, came to an end as we ran under a great stone arch of some towering viaduct that loomed up through mingling mist and compelled emotion along with some kind of wild wonder about the trials of nature and man. We turned a corner, and as we gazed back across at this great solemn structure from another age, with heads full of awe and hearts full of dream, we crawled up the last bit of hill, to where we'd disembark.

We disembarked creakily as the carriage was creaky and the ambient noise near inexistent, lending a creak, however small, its moment in the spotlight. The coach driver jumped down and pulled our affairs off the back of the coach with a slide, a thud, and a small grunt too which carried no less dignity but rather rounded off the choir. Tilting his hat to us with a strangely knowing smile, he stepped back on to his coach and gave the reins a crack. Then to the sound of snorts and whinnies, clip clops of hooves, and creaking wheels, the trundling took to track again to brave the moors once more. We stood alone in the dying light next to our cases which stood also, on the floor, and we watched the carriage disappear down the darkening lane and away under the big arch. I felt glad then that we were here, in company, and heading onwards, and weren't alone, not here, heading backwards under the descending night. My companion got a little notebook out and made a note; I'd noticed he liked doing this, although what he was noting, I didn't know. I felt slightly jealous though and thought that perhaps I must get a little notebook of my own in order so that I too could make small notes about things, the subjects of which my companions could be left ignorant of. Then we walked a short way and stepped onto the platform where our journey would begin.

We waited for some time after we arrived at the station, and it was cold. But it was a particularly satisfying station, along with its surroundings in general, in keeping with our journey which had been good despite a disappointing start in a town with a canal and some mills that were sombre and lacked sanctity, but yet reminded us of poetry without remembering why. The station itself stood alone, comprising just one platform and small station house that together had been tasked to hold steadfast a great frontier of civilisation. Victorian lampposts stood in stately rank to line where we would wait, the last fading into the mist that came with the approach of night, leaving warm fuzzy glows that dotted down and away to where beyond our realm of view. We could still hear the grouse calling into the dusk from their little grassy tussocks, or heathered rock perhaps, and we felt, standing on this station platform, like we were on a little island that battled to keep the night and unknown at bay.

"What didn't he want to know..." my companion murmured as he gazed across to the darkness that reigned the other side of the tracks.

"I dunno," I murmured back as I gazed in similar fashion, "maybe it was the sheep thing — could have been loads of stuff though..."

Several other passengers were already waiting at intervals along the platform. It was too dark to get a confident idea of their character and finer details, but we could make some initial deductions. One roundish figure stood with a small gleaming briefcase and puffed a pipe, coughing intermittently, but holding no apparent fear of smoke or lack of luggage space. There were a couple of women further up, enhanced by copious attire including long dresses, hats, handbags, frills and other accessories here and there which we didn't know the name of. They talked and giggled with little mercy for silence or stillness. One lone man stood on our other side, choosing to pace around with frequent pocket-watch checks while looking up and down the tracks. Through the dark and mist further down you could see one or two silhouettes and cigarette glows battling the platform's cold air, but little of the figures that were responsible for them.

It was Djako, the companion I travelled with, who came up with the train tickets. He told me that he'd found them on the floor somewhere, and though I hadn't really believed him, I liked the thought of embarking/escaping on a new venture and so I'd accepted the idea nonetheless. It wasn't long before, on a mountainside somewhere, that his figure first appeared to me — in a blinding flash from nowhere — and this apparition still seemed haunt me now, in the form of him. I often questioned, when I looked at him, whether roaming there that fateful day was a monumental blunder, as unfortunately he'd claimed he too was taking that same way, while not *joining forces* wasn't optional. So my mountain detox full of self-discovery was laid waste to there and then, this new companion in its place.

Though maybe he had a positive role yet to play, could be the optimistic outlook, I'd been thinking as I accepted the ticket; *like a destiny thing from a tale, such as in the guise of this new journey he proposed.* And whether trust in such a stranger was well-founded could be just another question to be pondered, while recalling his tall silhouette looming through the mountain mist, before the great blockish jaw and carefree lollop came, as his grinning face broke cover and fixed direct upon me. A sight which *seemed to suggest a little bit more Neanderthal within when taking his mental capabilities into account also*, I'd pensively proposed to him one time, although he didn't agree, even if he was apparently things like half-French, half-English, and half-American — where the maths just never seemed add up. And be it salient or not to this contentious point, I'm familiar now with his tendency for exaggeration/not telling the truth.

"You brought a big case." Djako said, while eyeing up the brown trunk that stood on the platform next to me.

"Yeah," I replied, eyeing up his case in return which comprised proportions that looked annoyingly correct, "thanks for your commentary — I've always had a weakness for overpacking and while I'm well aware of it, I can't stop doing it."

"Maybe it's a medical condition," he continued, "you know, something psychological…"

"Could be." I remarked, eyebrows cocking up, "Your bag looks to possess exactly the correct dimensions for a trip of this nature — I suppose you've had the psychological training or simply never had need of any. So well done there."

We continued with some more rather enjoyable small talk until, at last, the train arrived. Exactly on time mind you. We heard it coming due to the customary toot a steam train of its nature seems to make just prior to arrival at each of its station stops.

"Ahhh," Djako sighed, "that's a heartwarming sound, don't you think?"

Yeah it is, I thought, *although maybe heartwarming isn't quite the right word...* but I couldn't think of the right one. And then I thought I must ask the guard if I could have a go at pulling the cord responsible for triggering this sound at some point; of course, I could pretend I was interested in the mechanism so as not to seem childish. The train came to a gradual standstill along with a whole orchestra of other mechanically melodic noises and as the smoke cleared, a majestic black engine stood before us, followed closely by a train of carriages.

As those of us on the platform waited for the signal to board, we could feel the customary tension as we all pretended to be calm while privately preparing to implement our pre-planned boarding and seat/luggage-storage acquisition strategy. But with the signal come and stepped on board, chaos seemed imminent upon seeing the carriage was designed in a traditional compartmentalised format — something I'd had less experience with. However, strategy simplification seemed all that was needed: identify empty compartment (midway through carriage so users have option to continue after seeing part-occupation), enter, put luggage in most easily accessible position (ignore that shorter/weaker users may have difficulty accessing the higher positions), take the best seat. Well this was successfully implemented, so we sat back, and waited on the edge of our seats as forlorn stragglers boarded and wandered down desolate carriage corridors hoping to find place while not inflicting guilt upon themselves for shattering some innocents' dreams of a personal compartment. You could see them through the compartment door window, some looking stressed, while those foul players who don't care about shattering dreams looked just fine, or even slightly content.

A whistle sounded through the open window from somewhere out on the platform and the train started to move. I looked out of the window as the train pulled away from the station and wondered why it was open because it was cold. The cold air felt good though; it was mixed with smoke and wet mist and flowed into the little warm compartment from the blackness outside, and it felt like two worlds meeting, when, just for a moment, you felt some energy you didn't know, and were unsure of which world you were more. In silence, we endured a little this battle of worlds and the uncertainty it inflicted upon the air, giving things of no reason some reason maybe, and rendering points of uninterest points worth a thought, and as senses teemed you could think there was something more to the world than perhaps we'd been told.

"Feels good the air doesn't it?" Djako called out after some time.

"Yeah..." I replied in pleasant surprise along with some more involuntary eyebrow cocking.

"Yeah, that's why I opened the window," he said happily, "I knew it would."

FfffssshhhhLACK!

The window between the two worlds was broken suddenly and we were left alone in the lamp-lit compartment as we raced on through the night; just a yellow dot to an onlooker or some flying bird, along with a row of other very similar yellow dots, rolling on to somewhere that would be our next place to roll on from. Djako sat back down having closed the actual window, which to break it had no licence, and arranged himself into a train-seat napping position, put his hands in his jacket pockets and pulled his cap over his eyes. I decided that meant further conversation was redundant and so I pursued a period of reflection in hope of finding some satisfaction before doing the same.

I woke up to the sound of the train clattering along, onwards through what I fancied emptiness, with only blackness outside. I wondered what time it was; then remembered to rather wonder why so humour this persisting prison that seemed built of time; surely only some kind of over-meddlesome marauding mind would fashion such a killjoy with such matter. So sighing resignedly and drifting back to sleep, I thought I was dreaming when I heard someone's call; the train guard's presumably; asking about tickets. *But who asks for tickets in the middle of the night?* I considered to myself. Well it was indeed the guard and he turned out to be an exceptionally jolly one which I supposed was nice. Because there were always those who would grumble and kick legs that protruded into carriage corridors as they patrolled their territory that was the train. So I nodded, reassured, and felt grateful to be served by the guard in situ. He knocked on the compartment door window.

"Tickets please!" he repeated.

I gestured to him so that he might enter.

"Late to be checking tickets isn't it?"

"Huhhuuu yes!" he chuckled.

I was expecting more of an explanation but he seemed to think this sufficient and so I contemplated while debating the nature of his character.

"So really," I said while searching for my ticket, "why so late at night?"

"Perhaps I'm a night person," he replied, "which would result in my activity predominantly taking place during the night."

"Well yes," I countered, "but what about customer care?"

"What's that?" he said with what I thought might be a smile but wasn't sure.

Since I couldn't tell whether he was joking and because nature-debating still raged on to cloud judgement, I decided to query no further.

"We should do this more often." he said as he turned to leave.

"What?" I contemplated and then said.

"Nighttime chats." he replied in a matter-of-fact manner, and then left.

I woke the next morning wondering if the nighttime train

guard encounter had been real or not. I liked thinking myself a rational person and so decided it was but also that it might not have been. Continuing then to look out the window, mountains came to fill the pane, towering and rising all round to triumphant unconquerable peaks adorned with pure white snow like some capes of invincibility. The temptation that has come to so many other fallen and unfallen climbers, to climb and conquer, came to me for a short while until a voice I didn't recognise spoke up.

"Yeah, conquering mountains is just the same as winning a chess game, running the fastest in some athletic event, or being the best tennis player the world has ever seen — not really relevant. In fact, don't all these *triumphs* just suggest attention seeking, obsession slash wasted effort, and a little bit too much ego?"

"Hmmm," I replied, eyebrows cocking up involuntarily again, for the third time now in a disturbingly short space of time, while identifying this new compartment perpetrator, "yeah interesting…"

While I liked the point, I did at the same time suspect this ideology risked being a dangerously negative attitude, which, while appealing perhaps, if pursued, might lead to increasingly high levels of life dissatisfaction if not managed properly. The man seemed happy with my response though and so I decided not to voice any secondary concerns at this point. But yes, I decided to stay on the train in our cosy compartment rather than to attempt any conquering just then. N.B. Just to make sure, I ran a simulation of climbing and conquering the highest mountain visible in my head, and after successfully completing the challenge and returning to the train, I was quite happy along with hardly a scratch to bear.

"What about running a simulation of climbing the highest mountain in your head and allowing yourself to successfully conquer the mountain this way?" I found myself blurting out as the feeling of success had taken hold, "Perhaps this could give the self-satisfaction necessary while keeping attention seeking and effort to a minimum?"

After a short pause which nearly became an awkward silence, the man confirmed, in the nick of time, that he thought this was *an excellent idea*. However, at the same time, Djako laughed and said it was stupid, which was annoying, but we weren't laughing so I reckoned that his ridicule fell short.

"Right let's get to breakfast!" he continued happily while rubbing his hands.

So stepping out and shaking irritation off as best one could, our compartment door slid shut behind us and we moved to discover the train that would be our home for some time to come.

2

THERE WERE TWO lines of them, running in disciplined symmetry down the carriage we came to breach that day. Cloaked in white cloth and permitting clear passage only through a slim corridor that held fast the central ground, any frequenter would be well guided, not least for the green glass lamps that stood atop the brink of each, waiting to be switched on so they could shine. These fine tables marked a great hallway we'd come to call the dining carriage, for this is where we'd dine come day or night. And additional accessories/stuff was not lacking, the hallway boasting chairs, curtains, a long thin rug down the middle (we alleged there might be a name for that, but never checked), and to make things grand and more impressive, some chandeliers — possibly crystal, possibly not — never checked. And then just some more general stuff with questionable function. We took a seat, joined by the new anti-achievement man who we came to know as *Depressive Man*, or *D*, on the adjacent table since tables were only big enough for two.

"I wonder if they got an interior designer to do this?" Djako mused aloud.

"Hmmm, maybe," I replied, "it's pretty good."

"Nah," D cut confidently in, "it's just standard train dining-carriage design."

"Oh…" we both responded feeling somewhat taken aback.

"Yeah, look at all this stuff…" he sighed with an expression reminiscent of a smile, but a despairing one.

"What stuff?" Djako said.

"Stuff!" he snapped back, starting to look round wildly and wave his hands about, "Stuff stuff stuff!"

But then breakfast arrived to break rudimentary snapping and bring warmer, more comforting horizons to mind.

"So why were you two sleeping in a seating compartment rather than your room last night?" he asked us while tucking into a fried egg that broke into liquid to find bacon, beans, and other stuff.

And so warmer horizons melted away just as soon as they'd arrived as I looked at Djako questioningly while it dawned on me that this could potentially be a valid question. The expression of difficulty upon his face confirmed that it was.

"Hahuuu!" someone chuckled, "That was a funny sight!"

The train guard had appeared again to enjoy the scene.

"When you two are ready you can collect your room key and move in with your stuff."

"Great thanks," Djako answered while I looked at him

and wondered, "we'll collect them after breakfast."

"Yeah, my room was very cosy last night," D said while enjoying an amused smile, "nice not to be sharing too."

I looked at Djako again and wondered even harder as the horror evolved.

"Are we sharing?" I managed to ask, as, conscious of the overpacking situation, supplemental wondering about whether I'd have sufficient space for all my stuff reinforced heavy wonder already raging through mind.

"You sure are!" the guard chuckled back as he moved on through, "Hope you've not got too much stuff!"

I stopped looking at Djako then and we continued to eat breakfast in relative silence in order to mark the gravity by which this day had begun.

After passing the remainder of the day drifting around, thinking thoughts, banging heads on walls (mostly mentally) in dazes of mild-moderate frustration/reverie, and looking out of windows, salvation came at last in the guise of evening; this convenient development that comes with the fading of light and the obscurity it brings to make obscure that which would otherwise have no excuse to be obscure, rendering a continuous duty to understand, discontinuous.

Unfortunately though, an announcement shortly afterwards revealed that we were all to congregate in the bar carriage before dinner for a meet and greet. This didn't excite me as I didn't like these concepts, although it did Djako as he did like these concepts. Well we mingled and we met and we gret, to great effect, for after we knew more about some people than we did before. The two women from the platform with the excessive attire were some kind of dancers, and the roundish pipe man became known as the banker. Meanwhile, we discovered some of those responsible for the more elusive silhouettes that had lined the platform: a retired old gruff inspector, who liked to prowl and hold authority, and so prowling place and power were ceded, without bothering to resist; an old lady who liked reciting stories, and held an answer of kinds to everything it seemed, so she was wise; a man who was a mathematician and surely clever; a woman who was an artist and certain of her words; and a collection of others whom with we didn't get the privilege to mingle due to standard time constraints often suffered in such meet and greet situations.

The conclusion of this conjugation came none too soon, according to some, to mark dinner time, and so we went together, Djako, D, and I, to dine. We took up a seat at one of the small tables that lined the dining carriage. We wanted to sit together this time and so we conceived that one of us could pull up an additional chair which would admittedly be partially obstructing the central corridor but which also seemed like the only option at hand. Seeing the trouble that lay ahead for the user in the corridor, I quickly took up position in one of the official seating positions. Noticing my intent and sense of urgency, D quickly followed suit. Djako had yet to realise the disruption to user experience the unofficial corridor seat might offer and took up his position without protest or discontent. We looked at each other, D and I, and with a wry smile, relished a silent victory that had been achieved this night — perhaps the best form of victory there is.

The menus were already on the table which was good because we didn't have to wait for the waiter to conjure them up in an important fashion. An immediate problem displayed itself before long though, after already having overcome the initial problem of explaining to Djako why less choice on a menu was actually a good sign. Believing that red wine was most appropriate, I quickly suggested we took a bottle of this colour. Believing otherwise, Djako wanted for white without concession. Meanwhile, seeing the discontent growing in the ranks, D leapt on the opportunity to exacerbate the situation and claimed to want rosé, although I suspected he preferred red or white because no one real prefers rosé. With this conflict of apparent interest, after some dispute, we finally came to a compromise and ordered one bottle of each colour. This was on the condition that the chooser of their colour drank seventy-five percent of their colour in order to prove that they really did want that colour. While this compromise seemed fair, it had the effect of yielding cognitive dissonance by the end of dinner and so we went on to order whisky as it seemed like a good idea. This resulted in an increased level of cognitive dissonance and a series of debates that are difficult to clarify. After a while we were asked to leave the dining carriage, as apparently it was bedtime. It had been an excellent evening though and I think we all agreed we might be friends, in a way.

Some days went on to pass, blurrily and forgotten, where not much continued to happen save the continued ticking of time and clank of train. Until it was a new morning of note, when desire to get out of bed was surpassed, by desire not to get out of bed. This wasn't a cosy desire where bed feels just too right and sure to abandon at least for a little while longer, nor a Sunday morning's soft desire when satisfaction reigns and the right to stay in bed precedes lazy breakfasts and walks in crisp country air when breathing alone seems special. No, it was a desire to stay in bed because nothing of interest waited outside of bed. No sight, or word, or pending taste; even one that tingles. And a smiling face, some new-found sound, or thought that seemed so true; these were just trivialities then, small details paling in amongst the void. So to take refuge in bed and dream bleary-eyed, trouble-toned dreams that'll dance in and sidle out of a flailing mind that's grasping with poor grip, seemed requisite; where one might grapple bare air through which ideas and inspiration only come to pass before passing on to somewhere that knows better. So after some unsatisfactory lying in, at last I heaved myself out of bed as myself seemed heavy and in need of heaving. After a wash of face and brush of teeth, I started wondering what had been dreaded so from beneath the safety of the sheets and made a note not to dread again while already planning to disregard it. Meanwhile, the compartment door slid open.

"Come on!" Djako exclaimed, having returned from breakfast, "Let's go patrol the train!"

"Nah you go ahead," I muttered, "I'm going to stay here for a bit — I'll come find you."

Whilst dread had retreated, I hadn't felt ready yet, I don't think, to brave the world in such entirety just then. So the door slid shut again and I stayed here for a bit in this little sleeping compartment that had gladly accepted the role of headquarters for an unspecified duration of travel. I sat on my bed and listened. There was the noise of the train clanking smoothly along the tracks of course, reminding us of our moving from place to place and from before, to now, to next. But I didn't want to think too much about destiny just now and so I found myself enjoying the simple, innocent sounds that gave a timid backing vocal to this relentless sound of destiny. Faint clickings as doors were opened and closed, giving eager patrollers post-breakfast access to the train, or perhaps returning defeatists entry to post-breakfast sanctuary. And then muffled voices that accompanied this procession as users met and gret in-corridor, or gossiped excitedly, or irritably, or perhaps just requisitely on their way with friends or foe. The odd *phhhhwwwuppp!* as someone slid a window open to feel the air outside come eagerly in, to crisp and slice laziness out of lazy old air. And then silence again with just the smooth clanking soloing on, untroubled by lack of backing support, or the pressure of performing for us all. I moved to run the bathroom tap and water gurgled freely out before disappearing and so asking more to follow. The mirror above the sink demanded a mandatory glance, holding no concern for will and other plans it might have harboured. Seeing myself listening to the water I wondered if I was strange, or lost, or happy, or sad. I searched my eyes but couldn't read them like I might another's. Maybe they were hiding from me, or me from them. Or maybe there was nothing to read. I decided to splash the running water onto my face as a solution to the heavy train of thought, and this simple remedy worked, because it washed away the jumbled way I'd come to find myself upon, and brought things back again to start. So I breathed in deep and out again, found question had retreated somewhere, and wagered I was free then, to go and join that clown and patrol this damn train.

Later on, after lunch had been brought and broken into bits to the satisfaction of mind and body, the artist suggested an afternoon activity. She was very keen to give everyone a painting lesson, or *exercise that would bring us back into the depths of our minds and soul*, as she liked to describe it. While no one seemed particularly enthusiastic, we all agreed, as it turns out there isn't much else to do on trains or when there is no job conjured up to provide diversion from demise by thought. She wanted us to focus on figure painting. One of the dancers volunteered for this, although so too did the banker. So we had a vote to let democracy decide which candidate was most appropriate. The banker got annihilated and decided to say he was discriminated against. But we just said *yeah obviously you were — your physical form is rubbish when compared to that of hers*, and agreed how good the collective thinking was. When it transpired that it would be a relatively nude figure painting, the banker seemed relieved, while Djako was looking pleased.

"What are you looking so pleased about?" the banker asked him, which quickly brought his face to blush.

"Yeah inappropriate..." I said while feeling basic nature taking hold of me, and so parrying with words that people could hear, "inappropriate…"

Her companion, the other dancer, looked slightly annoyed/jealous that her counterpart would be on detailed display and receiving most of the attention that afternoon. The old wise woman who we knew as *Enlightened One*, aka *Enyone*, said something about leaving things to the imagination, and these meaningless words seemed to comfort the dejected dancer as she took up her pen in arms. I took up my pen next to her and began to paint on the pad I'd been assigned. Djako and D sat in front of us which was nice as I could check I wasn't doing anything wrong with my painting. A little while later, the dancer next to me hit Djako on the back of his head with her brush — something about certain body parts being drawn out of proportion. Djako quickly started to adjust his painting. I got a glimpse and had to admit he might have taken liberties in areas, which was my official stance when the dancer asked me to second her accusation. Luckily I was still on the face, and so I made a mental note to continue down with a notable lack of liberty.

"It's called artistic impression." D continued lazily with a surprisingly nonchalant attitude.

I wondered why he was risking himself in such a relaxed manner, before paint was sprayed liberally onto the back of his head along with the painting before him. He looked disappointed and surprised that this had transpired, which was in itself a surprise. Djako laughed and I did too; I think we'd all decided that it was good fun this business of soul-searching through painting, and we continued for the rest of the afternoon in high spirits.

At the end of the day paintings were judged and categorised from best to worst which some thought wasn't very in keeping with the soul-searching that had been pretexted, but someone had to be the best and someone the worst, and only a vote could shed truth onto things. The banker surprised, pulling through with the most votes while D and I were last. I decided to try saying that I felt discriminated against to see what recompense might come, but people just said *yeah obviously you were — your artistic capabilities are rubbish.* Anyway, that's collective thinking for you it seems — low ability to make the correct decisions while taking discrimination off the scale — since yes, mine in fact showed by far the best underlying potential. Because yeah, apparently mine possessed a notable lack of liberty, but there were myriad factors involved here which no one was interested in exploring; why if only those who understood art were the sole and rightful voters, it would be a different painting hanging on that dining carriage wall, because it was the winning painting that earned public display rights with no credence given to the other ones.

I went on to mull about that vote and the way it should have gone while eating dinner on slow evenings when gazing lacked direction and so would wander to the banker's lesser piece that hung without remorse yet confirmed to me repeatedly these people's plain great failings; their voting overrun by immorality and incorrectness grace their wild discrimination and poor schooling. And this convenient confirmation brought some solace at least, to the long nights that stretched ahead each time, which stayed a persistent gnaw that would otherwise play upon the mind.

3

AFTER PASSING SEVERAL days and nights subject to a steady gentle rocking and fleeting country flicker by, we stepped off the train one afternoon to feel the sturdy crunch of gravel underfoot, while the view cared not to fleet. And this was welcomed with more welcome than expected, before this newfound satisfaction slipped away, since such trivial change in circumstance could never be upheld at the forefront of one's mind.

"Everyone off?" the guard called as he retreated back onto his train, "Good, you're staying at Hotel House tonight, and enjoy yourselves... it's haunted!"

Chuckling, he nodded his head and shut his little window, hastening to direct his train onwards. There was no platform here, but there was a track that wound across and up a little to an old-looking hotel; a small mansion it seemed, with crescent windows, sprawling wisteria, and upper stories, reminiscent of a place where ghosts lurked and watched from hidden nooks and dusty corridors. The train pulled away as the scuffling of luggage and disparate grumblings died down and the hotel was considered from afar. We wondered a bit where the train was going just as we wondered at this hotel. It looked out of place, like some great painter had returned to paint it onto the once-rural canvas it now sat nestled upon, or like an orange on a tree of apples. Not dissatisfying, nor jarring, but rather thought-provoking, transfixing, and slightly confusing to mind as it took some time to make the place fit and assure itself there was no trick or hallucination at hand.

We marched up the track that wound up to the open gates and stepped across the threshold into this foreign Eden that sat amidst another more authentic Eden, because these forests and green mountain slopes had been here and breathing long before this questionable pretender which could not seem shake a sense of falseness. Djako and I were first to reach the big doors that loomed a bit, and so I turned to D and the others behind us to look for our next move.

CLANG CLANG CLANGGG!

"AHHH!" I cried inadvertently, suffering a temporary loss of control.

Djako looked at me contentedly while effecting another *CLANG!*

So, he'd gone straight in for a confident ringing of bell having decided discussion or camaraderie reassurance unquestionably unnecessary, even though this was a strange place, with looming door, and ominous-looking over-sized bell; a combination which surely demanded otherwise.

"You idiot." I muttered, giving him a look of contempt.

He looked back untroubled and an agreeable usher answered the door to usher us in, leaving him unquestionably triumphant.

We were told to make ourselves comfortable in the lounge area where a log fire emitted its mysterious rays of immense comfort and soft armchairs beckoned. It was early afternoon though and the sun was shining, asking all those within whether they should in fact be un-within. An exploratory walk felt requisite, and so Djako, D, and I left the others for the unknown. We walked out the gates and up a track that led into the woods behind the hotel, and as the pace stabilised, and our walking found its rhythm, a spot of spare time was afforded us, permitting things like observation and clear thinking to roll smoothly into place. And following this new state of play, it became apparent that Djako was carrying some fishing equipment; our spare-time observation skills proving proudly far from novice.

"What's that about?" I asked, "Where d'you get that?"

"Hotel gave it to me," he replied happily, "said there was a lake up here — a perfect spot for fishing!"

I looked at him; I didn't like fishing. Well we came out of the woods that led onto some fell and yes, there was the lake, an excellent looking lake. He set himself up excitedly and as he did so, we watched. I wasn't in the mood to sit and witness the hours that would follow. The cirque we'd found ourselves within consisted of a shallow bowl with steep mountain slopes rising round on all sides. On the other side of the lake I could see a small path making its way up the hill before disappearing into rock and slopes above. It was a temptation to be resisted with little to no resilience. And so an urge to climb up and find the lonely summit above this small lake was succumbed to gladly. I therefore told Djako that I'd always found fishing boring and pointless unless you were planning on eating the fish afterwards, and left him there by the lake. D had agreed, so we strode along, excited perhaps, at the thought of being a little lost out in nowhere here so that we could be given clear objective, even if just for this moment, of returning home safely; we could know where we had to get ourselves, physically, in order to succeed this day. We wandered along and I considered how it was easier to know where one might want to be physically in comparison to where one might want to be mentally.

We ambled, scrambled, puffed and scuffed, and before too long we'd reached the ridgetop where the snowline began, running on into mist and mountains unknown above and beyond us. I could see two pairs of footprints leading away to the above and the beyond us, to the high places unknown, and wondered what might have become of their benefactors. A strange but familiar sense of longing came; a longing for not know what exactly, but a longing nonetheless. I expressed my temptation to follow them up, but D happily reiterated his first words the time we'd met in the little train compartment, and laughed such ideas off.

"Haha, they'll climb and climb to the sky," he confidently announced, "but yeah, the sky will be no one — just some clouds and the sound of their mind."

So I hung my head a bit and accepted defeat. I did choose to reciprocate though, reiterating some of my first words to him regarding simulation strategy and suggested we do a bit of simulating as we made our way down from the ridge. He agreed.

"In addition," I added as we dropped from the ridge to descend, "perhaps mountain climbing has a further function — another very different function to attention seeking and ego-satisfying, as you venture to suggest."

I checked his reaction before continuing, to make sure that he was listening.

"Perhaps through taking a walk in the wild, by losing where we are physically, we are paradoxically un-losing where we are mentally as our purpose in time is now clear since for this moment at least, we must re-find ourselves, and we know how to do this: by returning ourselves safely, to where physical safety be."

"Hmmm..." he hummed back pensively, "yeah if only mental safety was so evident too, on some map we drew, or down the country lane to where the weathered signpost stands — perhaps a little leaning, and almost faded now — but still directing nonetheless."

"Well this ability to render ourselves out of place physically could always be a solution to our being out of place mentally." I continued, "There's little less out of place than sensing the safety of an old pub after a long walk or waiting on a lonely country station a train will come to carry us away from as the night is falling and the light is fading and the woods are getting dark. So if we keep moving from place to place, from where we are to where we will next move on from, to our destination that is our safety — our short-term destiny — a destiny which is known — can be known it seems, in these circumstances in which we place ourselves, then can we tame incessant tinglings of bareness and frustration that roam unchecked inside us? Can we deceive ourselves into believing we are serving purpose, succeeding in our trials, finding safety and ourselves again and again? Maybe to know our destiny is all our minds ever wanted... or rather to consciously, and constantly, conceive and achieve our destiny if this is a different thing at all. Should we place ourselves in circumstances where destiny is knowable then, conceivable and achievable, even if artificially so—"

"Errrhurrr... have you quite finished?" D interrupted loudly to bring a returning of reality, "Do you have low blood sugar? Perhaps there's a stone over there with a sword in it for you..."

His interrupting had turned to satisfied chuckling.

"You idiot." I retorted slightly pained, and pushed on, yes, pushed on to destiny.

Fish was on the air as we shuffled ourselves back in through the porch of the hotel just as dusk was done. The sounds of evening and merriment drifted through to us as we stood cold and untended in the abandoned foyer which felt forlorn and to be mourned. And it seemed contagious, so after a little stand and an involuntary sigh that felt defeatist, we let loose wet boots and sidled through, to the dining room, which was warm and unmistakably sanguine.

"What's that?" I asked arriving at Djako's table.

"Fish."

Fffuck! I quickly thought.

"What," I continued cautiously while gesturing out the window, "that you caught up at the—?"

"The lake, yup!" he happily finished for me.

"And it's just wonderful!" the dancers tittered, and the banker wittered, and some others simpered, as they all chuckled and raised their glasses to toast each other in delight.

I wondered how much he was enjoying his feeling of satisfaction as he made his triumphant reply to a fishing comment I'd afforded him earlier that afternoon.

"Careful of the bones." I said while gazing around the dining room.

"Thanks."

At this point it became apparent that everyone was eating fish and he'd supplied dinner for the whole train plus what looked to be the hotel staff that evening. With no choice but to accept this silent victory of his, I joined his merry table and started to eat mine too, along with D who'd gone all broody; thinking things good or bad, who knew. *But what did it matter*, I thought, though slightly darkly, *even if he was considering how he might have been better off staying fishing with this clown down by the lake.*

After dinner it was time to discover our rooms before resuming the merriment the evening was aspiring to. Sleeping arrangements would match those of the train and so Djako and I began and then quickly completed the long walk to reception. The receptionist took our details, did some scuffling followed by key presenting, and looked at us.

"You've a beautiful view from your room you know." she smiled and softly said.

We looked at each other, the long walk becoming short, with some degree of glee, possessing now the received knowledge that our room might be better than a high proportion of the other rooms our travelling companions would find themselves occupying that evening. As we mounted the stairs however, I experienced a disheartening thought, remembering the sun had made its farewells some time ago. I'm not sure Djako had endured this secondary knowledge yet though, because as we entered the room he hastened over to the window and threw back the curtains triumphantly. There was a silence then, as he held his back to a silhouette in the light of the doorway that was mine, and gazed out into the black. I watched, wondering of the expression upon his face, and the thoughts he might have known for those moments he stood gazing. Time waited for a time, for him to say something. He didn't say something though; he just stood, gazing, his cloaked shoulders heaving steadily up and down in the silence. He turned around at last and suggested we go down for a drink. *Not a bad conclusion*, I thought. So I agreed, and not looking back, we slinked out, to leave the dark room that lied alone.

"What have you two been doing?" D asked us over his merry tumbler of whisky as we rejoined the evening down in the lounge.

"Just admiring the view from our room." I said.

"But it's dark outside!" he laughed, looking at the banker

he sat with to encourage collective scorn, finding flaws in things as usual.

I checked Djako's status, but his eyes were glazed over and transfixed by a drinks menu he'd conjured, and so decided not to respond directly but moved on to another, more salient subject.

"Yeah, D and I were talking about losing ourselves earlier in order to find ourselves again, although I'm not sure he really understood, yeah just to summarise, it was something along the lines of..." I continued, with a quick glance at D and clear of throat, "in order to become found, one must be unfound, lending a confounding improbability to the sentiment of satisfaction in the acquisition of destiny. For once destiny is realised, one is no longer unfound, and so cannot aspire to become found. So then that which is yet to be, can only be commenced by rendering oneself unfound again, in order so that we might become found, again. And so goes the insufferable cycle of destiny, which I'd propose we might call life."

What my current cross-table adversary hadn't calculated for was that I'd spent some time (ages) reformulating my train of mountain-inspired thoughts into a much more succinct and impressive passage of conviction that was designed to blow everyone away, and indeed did, earning me a good deal of admiration, while at the same time, a high level of scorn for D who I suggested had been dismissive of my thoughts, and actually quite hurtful. So I gladly enjoyed the revenge I took on him as he slunk back into the depths of his mind, probably making a note to take revenge back again at a later date. But everything was all too merry now, and I was basking in too much the delight of revenge now, to worry about scheduled revenges at later dates that were only *to be confirmed*.

We took another drink then, before taking a moment to observe ourselves sinking into armchairs that were accompanied by flicker of fire, dancing shadows, and the warm ambient noise of evening chatter and remark, all transpiring in a pub lounge that was traditional and where no detail might be changed. And the chatter drifted on around room…

"We weren't to know where, but wandering wildly up worn old corridors whence we thithered seemed a good place to start…" a voice floated over from a table nearby that urged one to go and join.

But then I had to swivel my attention round as more corners of chatter came to compete…

"My twenties was a decade of confusion, and my thirties that of attempted reconciliation with life and what would come to be known as false hope…"

Meanwhile, there were those from another end of the spectrum…

"Yes, he likes to be involved when we arrive before the subject of fish…"

And so turning quickly on…

"Would you like to hear the true story, or would you rather prefer the one with magic inside?"

"The one with the magic inside."

"But that story isn't real."

"What does that matter? It makes me smile…"

That's nice, I thought, *and they're reputed to be children no*

34

more, before the next snippets of chatter drifted over…

"…and then I saw god, he was walking where I wa—"

"—the smoked cleared! And we saw the ballerina three, gunned down dead across the bridge…"

Hmm, nice, I slowly thought in agreeable surprise. And then with glazed eyes I looked back to our own little corner in hope that we might compete well tonight.

"WHY ARE YOUR EYES ALL GLAZED OVER?!" Djako was shouting at me, really close up towards my face, with flecks of spit coming at me while slurping his drink.

A state of despair seemed imminent, but fortunately he soon found himself prey to a timely game of chess with the banker who talked of Sicilian Defences, Smith-Morra Gambits, counters here, absolute pins there, and other notions that perhaps crushed his mind just as he was crushed in his optimistic attempts to battle over this board that could be the world; the known, the clear, one and only world; of these two men that, although may be somewhat lost before and after, were lost no more for this magical moment of rule and objective that time afforded them now.

"Ha! He's sacrificed his rook on d4!" D laughed as the game progressed, "And for just a pawn!"

Wow, what a terrible move, I thought pleasantly to myself as I looked at Djako dreaming on and pushing forth to d4.

"Nah I've got a funny feeling I can hunt down his king!" he replied while maintaining a calm disposition that got the banker perspiring more than usual.

So as the banker swamped his handkerchief with a higher rate of brow-dabbing than any man who hadn't lost his cool would care do, D and I enjoyed some murmured

conversation along with intermittent observation of the surrounding room, whilst beside us graceful pieces pushed
carefree to meet their doom within this warring world that
raged awander, and everything seemed to be well.

A card tournament was proposed not long after as the evening adolesced and demanded new excitement and territory
to discover. *Canasta* would be the game at hand — a game
not many seemed to know, including ourselves. Well the
rules were read out by one of the dancers who had proposed
the tournament, over what seemed to be a long period of
time, because it turns out there are loads of rules in Canasta.
After she'd finished trying to explain the rules, numerous
among us agreed we couldn't remember most of them, particularly those at the start of the discourse. As dispute and
disorder over rules began to take hold, and dangerously
mutated versions of rules could be heard drifting through
the disarray, the mathematician stepped up in a heroic manner and perhaps the nick of time.

"Why don't we write them down on a big board," he suggested, "and display them in an upper quadrant of the
lounge area for all to refer to throughout the tournament?"

We agreed this was an excellent idea and so the manufacturing of the rule board was begun. This took a long time
and by the time it was finished it was getting quite late. But
determination to proceed with the tournament had become
rife throughout the evening's suitors and so we proceeded
to excitedly commence this wild game of rules and unknowns. We were divided into teams — teams of four in lieu

of the usual two, under the proposed grounds that strength in numbers could help with comprehension of play. D, the banker, and I found ourselves teamed with the inspector which inspired hesitancy due to the newfound pressure we thought we might find ourselves quarry to. Premature hesitancy proved well-founded as we sat down at our designated table to find our team name had mutated through the team-card manufacturing process.

"*The Dimbo Men*?!" the inspector growled at us, his hard stare piercing through us each in turn, "How has this happened!?"

"I-Iii don't know..." the banker stammered as his eyes agitated and his brow entertained some spasms.

Keeping quiet with D, I looked over at our opponent's team name — *The Canasta Bastards* — and wondered whether they'd had trouble too, though their confident smirking seemed suspicious. We appeared to be facing the mathematician, the two dancers, and Enyone which led to further hesitation and which again was proven well-founded as we were crushed by these mysterious *Bastards*. The dancers kept going out early and apparently this was good. On our side the inspector kept banging the table and growling at us which wasn't very productive although we never aired our thoughts on this due to courage issues and also a high risk-reward ratio. Nonetheless, it turned out to be excellent fun as rules were struggled with, heated disputes were dealt with (sharing one hand of cards between two turned out to facilitate a lot of this), wine and whisky were met relievedly with, and then just because it was simply a good game. So amidst a melee of shouting, laughing, crying, and even sometimes screaming — perhaps as unforgivable mistakes were implemented or unbelievable suggestions of play were so wrongly ventured — cards flew, drink too, and so did words, both false and true, to bring fine culmination to a night that had deserved it.

We played *till sunrise* because we agreed we'd *play till sunrise*, at which point the party in the lead would be illuminated, by the sun only in part, and awarded their grand title in order to remind everyone else that they were definitely the best and most in warrant of respect. It should be noted that we moved *sunrise* forward several hours as some of the older party members felt actual sunrise was too late but did agree it had a more romantic, adventurous ring to it, leading to the preservation of this terminology used to mark the end. The party in the lead at this point were our original adversaries, *The Canasta Bastards* (whom I'd decided hadn't had trouble with their team name after all), presumably because seventy-five percent of their team had played before and already possessed a comprehensive understanding of the rules along with a well-maintained arsenal of crushing tactics. So they were given a well-deserved standing ovation and awarded their title that would distinguish them as the greater amongst us. And then it was bedtime, so we drifted off upstairs amidst disparate grumblings about dimbos, bastards, and deviously calculated evening-game proposition strategy.

It was my turn to throw back the curtains and admire the

view the next morning, so I did, and was greeted by a grey silent mist, lapping at the pane. Nonchalant and carefree it lapped as it idled and irked this place. I gazed out for a while, imagining a view that was there yet desperately un-reachable, and realised then, perhaps how Djako had felt the night before. I stood for a while more, transfixed by the sight, how things could have been different, and a relentless idea of how circumstances, meteorological preferably, may change so the view that was there might prove itself. It wasn't to be though, so after some heaving of shoulders that were cloaked by dressing gown, I turned to brush teeth and pursue other quotidian post-wake-up preparations, such as staring into the mirror in a variable manner. I caught sight of Djako, involuntarily, having fallen victim to a secondary effect of variable-manner mirror-gazing and the unantici-pated reflections it did bring. He stood alone at the window again, before he turned after a time when he looked some-what forlorn, and I understood an empathy for him then.

This dark day continued and drew itself out in a long manner; a gruelling manner that insisted on impressing a reminder of pointlessness and hopelessness on the small minds that would endure it with no choice. For the day had to be done, it had to be lived, and without doubt or con-scious recognition, we knew we had a duty to live it; perhaps for the next day, the day after, or a day that would come in a thousand years or more. Or indeed for a day al-ready passed, just now or an age ago.

The log fire burned with quite clear fatigue; it was tired of burning, and it was almost absurd — the wood didn't want to burn all over again this day, surely. The comfy arm-chairs weren't themselves; they weren't so comfy as they leant an ache to back, a crookedness to neck, and my word where were the footrests? The sun was shining but the rays, they were really quite bright. We were tired, heads were clouded, and the beckoning of the wild wasn't so beckoning as it should have been; perhaps it didn't try hard enough. So we festered this day and thought thoughts that were bleaker than they could have been, although perhaps not bleaker than they should have been. We pushed through dinner and through small talk that was smaller than it could have been as optimism and effort was smaller than it could have been. But still, perhaps not smaller than it should have been; this day perhaps warranted the defeatism that was, as we bowed now to show sign of respect for the loss we suffer, have suffered, and will always be destined to suffer. A respect that must be acknowledged, must be shown surely, so that we can together accept, and ultimately, half-gladly, embrace the lives we lead, however ruthless, unchosen, and so very rich in rawness they may be.

When social obligations were done, we sidled up to bed, one by one, or in twos at times.

"Don't forget your goodbye gift." the barman said to me as I followed the worn-out trodden trail to stairs.

He stooped below the bar and pushed a little teddy bear into my hands while looking into my eyes, a little more piercingly than standard practice might advise perhaps. I looked down as a strange sentiment secured itself some-where; it was just like one I'd had when I was young and smiled more.

"Where did you get that?" I asked, half afraid, half so uncared.

"Someone left it behind," he replied, "be more careful than the previous owner hmmm?"

So I continued up to bed, bear in hand, placed it on my bedside table, and hurriedly drifted off.

Pssshh... pssshh... pssshh.... I was woken by the sound of digging. It was coming from outside, below our bedroom window. I checked Djako, but he was unwoken. The sound of shovel entering gravelly earth seemed definite and distinctive. I lay for a while listening, waiting for a clue that might shed light upon the perpetrator of the act, but no other sound came, just the *pssshh*, the *pssshh*, and the *pssshh* again. It continued for an indeterminable amount of time that I determined must be minutes or hours and I started to think perhaps that it was simply imagined or dreamt, this cold repetitive noise. It wasn't a comforting noise; it was sharp yet dull, mechanically metalesque, and instilled a sense of dread and of space that was vast and empty with no sides to cling to. After extensive reflection I thought I should probably investigate — *who digs at this time of night but those that are up to no good?* I felt a bit too scared however, to go out, and so decided that to investigate fully would lend improper credence to paranoia and panic. Therefore, I softly stepped out of bed and tiptoed to the window to see what might be seen from this perch of safety. I drew a bit of curtain back and looked out. The noise was as ringing as ever, but only imagined glimpses of movement dappled frightened eyes that gleamed in a dark room. The digging stopped suddenly. So, heart jumping frantically, I worried I'd been caught looking and jumped, with heart, back into bed before anyone else might notice my unseemly sneaking around at such an hour. The digging recommenced then, but I drifted off, resigned to the bliss of ignorance.

I woke the next morning to some medley of bird song polluted by snoring from the other bed this room endured. Troubled thoughts swirled and lapped inside as though a bit of mist had come creeping in to irk when I hadn't been concentrating/conscious, or as though fallout from an atomic dream about radioactive mist and digging that had been both persistent and unaccounted for. Creaking from bed and returning to view the view one last time, a flash of teddy bear fleeted before me — an unforgiving face of dead glaring eyes, all abandoned, and covered in earth. I looked back wildly (mentally — but physically actually quite slowly and hesitantly to my surprise) and saw it was gone from my bedside table. Eyes darted (again surprisingly slowly/hesitantly in reality) back to the window and the below where the blessing of light let resume an investigation that had been foiled sometime earlier by lack thereof. But there was just neatly mown grass, all innocent and tidy, and it loomed through the mist at me and my window and our perch of safety that didn't feel very safe, but fostered guilt, or just a simple loss maybe, and for company had but an empty bed and a bare tabletop where there a bear once sat. Having thought about marching down to this neatly-mown grass to dig ferociously and reveal the tip of a great conspiracy that this Hotel House — this out-of-place place — was inflicting upon us all, I decided this could run the risk of myself being branded the insane passenger who finally lost it, and so I ambled broodingly down to breakfast instead where I'd join tables of fresh-looking faces and probably order some egg.

"I did some digging last night..." the inspector slowly started out as he stirred sugar in his tea.

I looked up from well-scrambled scrambled egg (it seemed they'd added cheese too — *a good idea*, I'd been thinking), stricken with anticipation and potential incoming enlightenment.

"...yes, I was in the *library* and fell across an old book — this place really is haunted you know. The ghost train comes, at night it seems, though I noted daytime comings weren't disqualified. Anyway, it steams in sounding its whistle which pierces through the mist, if misty. And the moon is always full, if night, so the way is lit for the lost souls it drops off. They come here to the hotel to find refuge on their long journey before pushing on."

"Ha, excellent!" Djako marvelled, "I wonder what they get up to on their stay?"

"Yeah, doesn't sound very haunted if they just stay here as regular well-behaved guests," D noted, "do they do anything scary or unprecedented?"

"Ahahummm... Iiii... didn't feel like reading on after that..." the inspector mumbled, "...the library was dark and things felt foreboding, and I was... alone, and it was time for bed... yes..."

"Ah even the bravest of us falter you know!" chirped the banker, giving him an encouraging pat on the back which the inspector seemed to appreciate.

And so on went the conversation with anticipation receded as troubled thoughts ebbed again and well-scrambled, cheese-enhanced scrambled egg became preference of focus once more.

When the clatter of breakfast and clamorous clinkings of a new morning were done and becoming distant, we took up arms (suitcases) and marched out of the ground's gate we'd marched through once before, onwards to the train, in column again, like some soldiers.

Welllll… we waited for some time at the non-platform (just some gravel/stones) until, at last, a majestic black engine arrived (exactly on time mind you, or so the guard would claim). And somewhat nostalgically, but unsurprisingly perhaps, it was followed by a train of carriages, which waited patiently, and with little choice, to be boarded. We debated that perhaps they'd been cleaned, these carriages, because they looked clean and gleamed a lot. And they inflicted a distinct air of pride and superiority over the featureless non-platform, which claimed not even a name, and that would accommodate them through little choice of its own. We found ourselves boarding with unmoditated haste; perhaps because we felt preference to be rid of this place that was so comfy yet so conniving, or perhaps just as we subconsciously implemented dysfunctional boarding/seat-acquisition strategies. And then, reacquainted with looks of satisfaction, we watched the out-of-place place go by and out of sight as the train and we, pushed relentlessly on, to Moscow or where glory surely be.

4

IT WAS NICE to be back on the train and pushing on, as we knew perhaps, unwittingly, that for as long as we pushed on, we would evade dark things that followed behind us, like thoughts, out-of-place places, or a state of safety and security that would hurl us into minefields of further thoughts centred around how we might escape this safety, in order so that a clear objective would be rekindled, and so we could claim to feel again, and believe ourselves to be more alive. Or perhaps it was just nice to be on the train again because it rocked, and it was familiar, and its boundaries were all findable and seeable, and because it rolled on so determinedly and unstoppably that nothing could stop us now as we surrendered ourselves, and our desire to control, to this machine that would guide us. Either way, onwards was the agenda that we could all agree on, without choice, or even need for choice, because we'd probably just choose wrong anyway.

And so some time went on to pass — days we thought, weeks possibly, or maybe months — which of us knew, or deigned still to fret, who could care as this train wrenched and split through to illuminate the whole notion as dubious and questionable, imploring us perhaps to reimagine how it was always born to be, and might be capable of being, outside the realms of calculation. So some time passed, and it was OK time sometimes, and less-OK other times, and overall it was just some time that bore us and that we bowed to bear.

It was another day that drew to a close when our compartment door clicked shut and I sat on my bed for a while. Isolated from the rest of the train, grace this compartment door and walls, I could feel alone again, and unsure. I lay down, and then seeing the little window with black behind it and the room reflecting from it, an urge came to open it. *Irritating*, I thought, *because I've just lied down*. I edged towards the end of my bed, and using my leg plus foot/toes I managed to slide the window down. Feeling I had won some time and effort, I felt a little satisfaction spring to life and a smug smile to accompany it. After this sensation had receded, the windmill resumed its rhythm though and whirred on as I stared out into the black above the half-open window, sometimes drifting to the familiar reflection below.

The train had been motionless for some time in this place along the tracks amidst this somewhere we didn't know. I wondered whether there were mountains outside, or a big forest that stretched out, housing its mysteries safely, away from the clutches of man. Or maybe a black lake shimmering in the moonlight, lapping hungrily at its shores, unsure of how big this world would be if it broke out and flowed somewhere. I heard a wolf cry, and panic-themed thoughts came to clamour clarity. Then after some consideration I re-assured myself that the train was wolf-proof and so reorganised initial clamour into dreams of how romantic it perhaps was. Yes, a savage romance, a troop of fur trappers making their way on some lost causeway to find gold up in the mountains as the wolf ran below on the cold hunt for survival.

And then somnolence was marked when came a thick brown, silent and swirling gently round like some worn-out cloud, with grey towers looming here and there — old bro-ken ones with no use no more but for catching awe. And here seemed reign a kind of smile, or what felt like could have been one, that saw broken rock fall defeated through rays of light and down dark slopes where things stumbled and scattered consciousness searched unity, to breathe a sti-fled cry that would bound between this place's barren faces and echo in the emptiness until someone beheld it and so set it free. I was walking alone, through an empty valley bounded by sides that rose up and disappeared into grey and there was thick brown all around, but not literally. Nothing moved, not even the water, which surely always flows, and broken rock fallen from high and dark deceptive places, lay cold, and animate no more. It was stuck, this place, and it was only me who moved and picked on through it. I thought at first it didn't know I was there, but then it struck me that I was stuck, in this one self-doubted moment, in this place that watched on and wasn't stuck at all.

The train was gently rocking when I woke, and the dim glow of reading light was still shining determinedly on, even without a book, or newspaper perhaps, to grant it purpose. Muffled voices drifted through from somewhere on one side, and from the other side only silence, while from the corridor someone was whistling *We Wish You A Merry Christmas* which was annoying because it wasn't Christmas. I pulled back the little curtains I must have drawn, to reveal the world outside. It was just black again, due to ongoing absence of sun and other light sources, so not much was revealed except one's imagination and maybe a little bit of one's self. Plus, be it less saliently so or not, actual reflection of oneself — absence of external light rendering a seemingly innocent window in fact dangerously more mirroresque due to physics or something.

"YO!"

Bang! Door smashes open. Isolation period was finished and return to company had come, yes, my roommate had returned.

CLACK, CLACK, CLACK!

"…YOU IN HERE?" he practically screamed while banging on the bedframe, "Come for a drink and a game of poker and a proper evening!"

It was strangely startling — disconcertingly comforting even — to hear this evermore familiar/annoying voice, and I noticed I felt glad. The suggestion came as a surprising respite to the company I'd been enduring that was myself, so collecting myself and de-clouding cloudy thoughts, I stepped out into the wild with a fresh dose of optimism.

"Good idea!" I said enthusiastically while rubbing my hands together due to the unexpected satisfaction that had sprung to life.

We marched down sleeping-carriage corridors lined with little lamps burning and flickering as the train rolled determinedly on through the dark, and we felt a real purpose just then, as we headed for the bar carriage and the card table we would huddle at with friends or foe to pass this beckoning night.

Djako threw down his cards in disarray and took another desperate sip from his depleted tumbler as the inspector chuckled hoarsely and reeled in his newly-won chips that clinked happily against each other.

"Ha!" D laughed as Djako made for a top up, "You're all out of luck tonight!"

"I don't believe in luck." remarked the mathematician who'd come to join us for the game.

"Is that right?" the inspector growled with a scornful stare, "What do you believe in then college boy?"

"He believes in numbers in order to make things fit." D answered for him.

"Yes well I've been getting into Buddhism too more recently actually," the mathematician continued, "to counteract or rather compliment the logic proposed by these numbers and so improving my chances of finding reason for existence by, say, at least two."

"Oh so what were your original chances with the numbers?" the banker asked.

"Wellll... near zero I suppose."

"Sooo... a rather misleading multiplication factor that could offer negligible results then?"

"Yes it could still do with some further augmentation through the addition of supplementary beliefs."

"Hmmm..." the banker hummed as his brow furrowed and he looked doubtfully at the man.

"Yeah I've been going down the morality route and hoping things turn out OK that way," I said, "although the near-zero problem you mention does loom sometimes."

"You could always believe in say, Christianity too, and that would help solve the zero problem." D replied, "Yeah, morality is basically just Christianity with the happy ending removed along with a few of the other questionable ideas, so you wouldn't have to do much there."

"Hmmm, yeah, interesting, but you know, how do you... get into tha—"

"Oh no but wait, you've got your destiny!" he interrupted with a cry and banging the table, "You could be destined for great things, great great things!"

"You shouldn't mock you know," Djako slurred, returning with a fresh whisky, "I'm planning on great things for myself and everyone else can do so for themselves too."

Unfortunately his support could only be half-appreciated because it was irritating.

"Oh dear," D continued, "let's hear what tosh mister America has got saved up his sleeves for us now..."

"You know, you could be great," Djako replied wagging

his drunk finger at him, "you could be mister optimistic man if you weren't—"

"Place your DAMN bets!" the inspector barked, "And stop BLABBING on, I thought only men and fine women played poker! What's wrong with this damn train!"

So somewhat flustered we quickly got back to it in order to be men or fine women, in case this was a good thing. And the evening wore on in good spirits as the bar carriage we placated this night was full and hummed an energy that seemed positive and true. We had our poker and whisky corner, and others had their own little corners/areas which were placated at respective corner/area level by vibrant conversation, soft murmurs, other games albeit lower quality ones, or just a series of affectionate looks and laughs between some lovers or non-lovers. And this combined placation crescendoed to contrive a place that was positive and felt good, perhaps as it held thoughts of necessary future action/uncomfortable unknowns at bay for one of those magical moments that aren't all so hard to come by, if guard is down, it seems. And all the while a violinist played on, having appeared without announcement or notice, but just appearing to play like no one we'd ever seen play, in a world of his own that was surely a good world; a world only he knew and so that must have been pure and true.

BANG! The carriage door flew open to reveal a silhouette standing in the doorway.

"Oiii! Youuu cccard players!" the unknown figure slurred at us, "You men and women, who drink and laugh, mouths agape, revelling in these debauched corners of this debauched carriage!"

"Just playing cards mate," D interrupted, "placating respective corners at a responsible level of intensity…"

"Someone's going to fall tonight — I've seen it — I was here playing cards with you," the silhouette droned on, "we sat here drinking and laughing, mouths agape, and we heard screaming, an empty room we found, ransacked, window agape—"

"What, like our mouths?" D interrupted again.

The stranger gave him a sneer and went on.

"Yes, we looked out, we were on a bridge across a valley we couldn't see the bottom of — too dark, too deep — just a river we heard running and—"

He stopped talking and looked up to the sky/ceiling. We waited, an air of anticipation noticeably rife, in the air, and a silence ensued throughout this once-placated carriage, with only the clink of cup, or chandelier possibly, and beat of train, breaking through it. We found ourselves regarding each other expectantly, wistfully, even a little woefully for a time, but time passed and then past the limit appropriate for airs of anticipation to last, and so we were obliged to return to normality and be like nothing was ever un-normal.

"Hahuuu!" the perspiring banker chuckled looking round at us, "He nearly had us there…"

And yet slapping down his royal flush, with mouths agape, due to cards in part only, a scream pierced through the little carriage.

"IT'S HHHAPPENING!" the triumphant, apparently ex-delirious stranger imperiously announced.

The air had changed, the carriage knew a new purpose

within; a call to arms was upon us that all succumbed and answered to with unreserved duty. Chairs grated back, determined white-knuckled hands pushed down on unyielding tabletops to facilitate rapid upright positions that could only mean business. Orders were barked, loose laces tied. These were the actions of men, and women to an extent, on a new mission; a new purpose had arrived and levity was naught but expelled, only to be caught and fondled again when it could be welcomed back with confidence, arm in arm with frivolity which we all knew had no place here and now. We found ourselves marching out the bar and down carriage corridors, feeling as a band of comrades might do on their way to the front.

"Room numbaaar? Room numbaaar?" the old inspector was barking.

Couldn't say..., *not sure...*, *who knows...*, and other cries and whispers echoed through the corridors.

"CHECK THEM AALLL!" the inspector bellowed, achieving a level of authority that no man could question.

Compartment doors were flung open, knocks reverberated up and down carriage corridors, distant shouts and clamours came eagerly to ear, while close ones came more deafeningly. With tensions risen and the air turned taut, carriage lanterns seemed to shine less confidently now, vulnerable to a puff of air that might just blow them all out (or a bout of short-circuiting if electric — never checked), though they flickered on nonetheless, through the thickness of uncertainty, to hold the fort, hold our train together as one no matter the cost. Then there came a new door and a *knock-knock*.

53

"HELLO?" someone called, "ANYONE THERE?!"

No answer followed by jiggle of locked doorknob.

BAM! Crack!

Door smashes open due to force of heavy-booted foot as train guard arrives disappointedly holding master keys aloft. Mouths agape, we crowd around an empty room, ransacked, and there it is, the window that imitates us, almost cruelly, because it's agape.

The train screeched to a halt on a bridge over a valley, so deep and dark we couldn't see the bottom. And as the stranger's words echoed round our heads, things seemed to be getting familiar now, disturbingly so. Because had he really foreseen such unpredictability? And if he had, what does that mean?

"Search the room!" the inspector ordered.

So we took on the role of newly-promoted constables with a fervour that we guessed must come naturally in such situations as we didn't usually have that much.

"And don't let anyone else in!"

Djako was placed on guard duty as he was big and could pretend to play the role a henchman might. The train guard arrived back from the engine room.

"No one's to come in." Djako said confidently and importantly, playing his newly-promoted henchman role.

"Let him in you imbecile," the inspector shouted, "it's the train guard damn it!"

So a stricken and disappointed Djako let him through.

"Well?" the inspector demanded, "Whose room is this?"

"Baaah... not sure sonny," the guard chuckled, "no records on this train — either lost or never forged!"

"No records?!" he spluttered back, "My God, I say again what's wrong with this damn train?!"

He walked over to grasp the window, knuckles gleaming on the cold frame, and looked out at the outside world in analytical, detectivesque thought maybe, or just frustration, or maybe just to look important and brooding like a detective should look.

"So what if they're just roaming the train and not currently present?" I ventured to say as I entered the investigatory probings.

"Well, what about the screaming?" asked the banker.

"Oh, mhmhmm, yeah that might have been me," one of the dancers said timidly as she peered curiously in from the corridor, "I thought I'd lost some cosmetics earlier."

"Hahaaa!" chuckled the train guard, "Looks like you lot might have been on a wild goose chase here!"

The inspector looked crestfallen and the rest of us undoubtedly felt the same. So we sidled back, feet dragging and heads half-hanging, to our little corner where we'd attempt to resume a placation that had been, and pass the evening away.

"OH MY LORD!" gasped the banker, "My royal flush has gone! My royal flush is gone! I had a royal flush — I slapped it down triumphantly when the scream came, and now it is no more!"

The queen of clubs had materialised and taken the once-cosy place of the queen of spades. I wasn't very keen to advertise my observations since I had a fair amount riding on this hand. In fact I think everyone had quite a lot riding on this hand because there wasn't much support for the banker's grand tale at all.

"Nooo you didn't! You fool!" D laughed, "You misread that queen of clubs for the queen of spades didn't you! Ha!"

I enjoyed D's theatrics. In fact, I think everyone did; a great feeling of solidarity had really taken hold all of a sudden in this unsuspecting corner of ours. So support for this treacherous banker was withheld unanimously, and quite rightly so, or so democracy might have put it then. The banker looked devastated, perhaps almost believing this story of D's/democracy, and so swamped with newly-inflicted self-doubt, and de-swamped of chips, he drew himself to get another drink. We watched him walk to the bar, smaller than before, and the once-great feeling of solidarity seemed to ebb away a bit into some feelings that weren't as pleasant and we sat as children for a while. And so just as the good are used and discarded, we discarded this man, this good man, a man we owed a debt; a man we would come to realise was perhaps no banker at all, and asked no debt paid, monetary or moral, or any other type of debt this world might muster to levy balance due.

"News people, news..." the train guard announced, returning and looking less jolly than usual although still dangerously unperplexed, "no one has claimed the room, the room has not been claimed."

"That suggests a missing person then." someone stated, a bit obviously, because the room was full of ransacked stuff.

The inspector stood up, so grim, and so full of resolve you wouldn't believe it.

"That's it, it's detective time..." he growled, "round two... and someone's going down!"

"What?" D said.

"Someone's going down." he repeated dramatically.

"Why's someone going down?" the banker asked.

"If there's been foul play then I'm going to catch the culprit and hence they're going down!" the inspector repeated while getting frustrated, "Now come on, let's move!"

So as the old inspector took up arms again, dreaming of catching mystery criminals, we dreamt too, reoccupied our constabulary roles, filed into line behind this great detective, and resumed the mystery of the window that gaped.

A little while later, after searching the room again to no avail, we found ourselves standing outside the train on this great viaduct that stretched across the deep and dark. And it was misty, and lanterns stretched down to light up with hazy glows the ghostly outlines of carriages that lined the bridge. And so yes, the combined series of preceding events accompanied by our physical surroundings and current meteorological conditions made this whole situation incalculably mysterious to all, except maybe one.

"This is a strange place," the inspector mused with a furrowed brow, "a strange case."

He looked at us darkly and we waited a while only for the tension to be broken by a familiarly loud voice.

"Right," Djako said, rubbing his hands optimistically, "what's the procedure slash plan now?!"

"I WILL GO DOWN INTO THE VALLEY BELOW AND IDENTIFY ANY EVIDENCE OF A FALLEN COMRADE!" announced the banker in a loud and resolute manner that perhaps shocked us all as he didn't seem suitable for missions such as this, and also it just sounded ridiculous.

"Are you insane man?" the inspector growled, "We're talking about vertical cliffs and drops here!"

"We could lower him down on a rope." suggested D who seemed to be enjoying developments.

"Ha!" the train guard laughed from his perch that he regarded us from, "That'll be a sight!"

"Oh well I think it sounds just heroic!" one of the dancers proclaimed while stroking the banker's arm.

He looked particularly pleased with himself and all the more spurred on as he determinedly pushed his round glasses up his nose, readying himself for action. I thought it was probably irresponsible of her to encourage him but at the same time it was an exciting prospect to be dangling him from this bridge, and since the others seemed to think the same, we began formulating the proceedings with no further ado.

Things started well as the train guard, who appeared particularly anticipant for the action to come, was able to procure some rope remarkably quickly that looked sturdy enough.

"How long does it need to be though?" the inspector sensibly inquired.

"Go get the mathematician." the banker snapped at Djako with continued fervour.

An agitated mathematician was woken and marched from his room.

"How long does this rope need to be to reach the bottom of the valley below?" the inspector demanded, "Quickly now man!"

We all waited expectantly as he looked around at us, perhaps with an expression of disbelief, perhaps wondering how he'd come party to such fanatics that played effortlessly with the boundaries of science, or perhaps with an expression of awe and respect for us heroes and our great operation; we could only serve conjecture here as it was difficult to see properly in the gloom. He sighed and shut his eyes, again in some kind of awe/respect maybe, or possibly despairing at the complexity of the sum, then he turned around and went back to his room or something. There was a short pause as the inspector stood holding his rope, mouth slightly ajar, and eyes glazed over while regarding the door the mathematician had just exited stage through. And the rest of us stood too, in a similar fashion.

"...That was weird, huh!" Djako chuckled looking incredulously at us all as he de-paused this operational glitch.

As time felt limited, decision beckoned while adrenaline levels were above average, so we quickly decided we'd estimate the rope length based on the sound of the river below. Djako reckoned he had a pretty good ear for sounds and therefore told us how to proceed here. Meanwhile we managed to develop a rudimentary harness for the banker using several pairs of large underwear and some bras. After what we all agreed was a really excellent team effort, we stood together around the banker in his new harness and congratulated one another.

Following a series of deep breathing exercises and meditative stretching pioneered by the artist who had joined the fray, and aggressively championed by our gallant banker who, by now, must have had the concentration levels of loads of numbers timesed together, the time had come.

"To the drop station!" the inspector called, "At the ready

men, we will not falter now!"

With this call to arms we took up positions by the edge of the bridge and peered over the wall into the foggy darkness of the valley below as the banker strapped himself in and prepared for his descent. There was an eerie silence as we waited, pierced only by the clinking of harness, the breathing of nervous company, and the odd crow's cackle, all through which the drifting mist mingled to complete a mysterious tapestry that was our world.

"Ready son?" the inspector asked, clapping the banker on the back.

"Yes..." he breathed, seemingly a little more nervous now ideas had actually progressed and transpired into reality.

"Let 'im down lads!"

So we let him down. We lowered him down from this great precipice; this starry stage on which our moment of glory would be known, where together in arms we'd achieve courageous things. He flailed a bit as we let him down, and didn't look very secure, but he gradually disappeared into the grey below along with his calls and so we felt more relaxed/confident as worrisome things became retreated nicely out of sight.

"Gently now..." the inspector purred as he kept his cool and inspired calm amongst the lowering party.

We continued lowering for a while and enjoyed a moment of serenity as we were gathered here together, in silence atop this bridge over nowhere in a place which could have been anywhere, and all we knew was the few metres of raw world around us on this old structure that gallantly stood through time.

"So how do we know when to stop lowering him and pull him back up?" D asked to break the peaceful pause.

"When he gives three tugs we'll know." the inspector replied confidently.

We waited together in silence and a few minutes passed.

"Can you tug on a rope when your weight is on it?" D queried thoughtfully.

With the inspector hesitating, we looked around at each other awaiting reassurance from one of ourselves. But none of ourselves came forward. The inspector nodded in the direction of the sleeping compartments.

"Go get the mathematician." he growled.

The mathematician was marched out again, and again making some expressions that looked awe-inspired, quickly confirmed the banker probably wouldn't be able to tug on the rope if it was taught.

"RIGHT, GET HIM UP!" roared the inspector, "GET HIM UP NOW!"

Serenity fallen away into the valley below, we found ourselves racing to aid the hoisting of rope, probably fuelled by adrenaline and a disappointing sense of disaster unfolding on our heroic stage that now teetered. It would be hard work pulling the rope back up though and I didn't want to burn my palms, so I accompanied D at the back with an aim to do slightly less work. As we hoisted, no sound sounded from the grey below in answer to our lonesome calls. However, before long he came, this man, this banker man; this man of resolve started to appear, although in a limp-like fashion, like a dead chicken or something, which was weird — *was he meditating again? Had he fallen asleep?* Well once arrived and back before us hanging in his harness, further observations revealed that he was indeed asleep/unconscious and also mega wet. Realisations dawning, we took some time to glance around at each other, hoping maybe realisations that had dawned weren't correct and could be un-dawned. This wasn't to be though. The artist therefore took up the gauntlet, rushing to apply several claps to back, and like magic, a splutter came forth to bring us from this dark dawn, to a slightly less dark one. He looked around at us all, just hanging there and bleary eyed.

"Angels..." he slurred with a faint smile, "...beautiful..."

The faint smile lingered on a bit too long to call healthy as he continued to look around at us and we waited hesitantly to see if he'd say something else. It seemed we'd collectively decided, telepathically, that it was best not to encourage him to think about what had happened below in case he came to realise/recall we'd drowned him in the river.

"Good man, good man," the inspector said giving him a pat on the back, "that's it, you're home now."

So as the banker was untied and appeared reasonably content with things, we enjoyed a wave of relief, and we all gave him our strong and total congratulations for completing his great mission with real style and fervour. And he seemed to take this pretty well.

"Come on everyone," the inspector called while clapping at us, "back on the train now, that's enough for today."

We were ushered back onboard, a bit uncertain about the success of the mission perhaps, and slightly confused about things as battle trauma and shellshock set in to the veterans we had come to be. The train guard had been clapping us too after witnessing events unfold from a prime seating position on his little perch that was the carriage roof.

"Do you want me to hold the train for you to have another go tomorrow?" he asked the inspector who brought up the rear.

"No, let's get out of here," the inspector muttered back as he stepped on board and shut the carriage door firmly behind us, "this is naught but a dank place, for men and dank dreams that merit no better than a casting aside into the dankest, deepest of pits."

"OK... sooo..." the guard continued tentatively as the inspector raised his furrowed brow to him.

"We're done with this damn place!"

"Jolly good!" the guard chirped, springing down from the carriage top.

With a blast of his whistle and a *HAAAAYYOOOO!* the train clanked into motion, to move on, and be rid of this bridge that held no mysteries, no, just deceitful tricks.

"Oooooh, the heroes are returned!" the dancers cooed as we filed back in to take a welcome seat and those waiting in the bar carriage looked at us expectantly, "You must tell us all about it!"

"All good, all good," the inspector shushed in a wrapping up manner, "everything's under control and we're pushing on now."

"Oh and we heard about your special mission," one of the dancers continued, diverting attention to the banker, "you brave brave hero!"

He recommenced with some more weak smiling and

would find himself subject to the dancers' attention and delicate caress for the remainder of the evening. Again, a useful occupation for him just now that might keep his mind from wandering to other, less appropriate horizons, like great operations on bridges, over valleys so deep and dark you couldn't see the bottom. In unsure silence, we looked at the cards before us which offered a stark reminder as they lay disarrayed across the tabletop, but with a royal flush that wasn't quite a royal flush still perfectly preserved. Then we looked up to each other, thinking perhaps, factoring in both this earlier card incident as well as the more recent one, that our debt to this man must be getting pretty high now.

"Maybe he's not actually a banker?" Djako said.

"Yeah who ever said he was?" D answered.

"Not sure…" I said after a short pause for reflection.

"Ha! So he could be a good samaritan who forgives all and asks no dues?!"

"Could be," Djako concurred, "could be…"

So, either way, we sang praises of him and successful missions for a short while to the receptive rear-guarders who'd successfully held the bar carriage, and then, after a well-earned nightcap, decided it was time for bed.

In the calm of the dark a short while later, finding myself quarry to some customary waiting-to-fall-asleep pondering, I thought what an excellent day it had probably been; all of us were alive and well, problems had been met head on, conquered, and overcome courageously to an extent, negative thoughts were currently docking somewhere obscure, voluntarily so, and all this world seemed really quite, well, marvellously mad.

5

WE WOKE TO ONE of those fine crisp mornings which dowse the world in splendour, and as we were sped so well through glistening sun-bathed country, light of heart we surrendered to a breakfast that would clink and clatter with greater intensity than that of a standard one. For a freshness about each of us lent free rein to clink and clatter cups and spoons and other clinky things as much as we jolly well liked.

We sat together, the banker, D, Djako and I, and made light of mysterious events we'd known on this strange train, enjoying chuckles and jibes that to and froed with ease across the playful space between us and the increasingly crumby sunlight-dappled tabletops. The inspector sat in good spirits, entertained by the artist, the mathematician, and Enyone, learning some wisdom perhaps, or just providing detective tips and reading extracts from a paper he'd conjured and rustled contentedly every now and then as he found a new page to scrutinise and tut upon, or to quibble and carp over under the promise of a young new day. And on our other side the dancers sat loudly with a couple we knew less well, but they weren't loud enough for our clinking and clattering which we found we were able to magnify with great short-burst precision to meet near-perfect syncing with the louder of their early morning efforts. Furthermore, the unsettling possibly delirious stranger from the night before was sitting way over the other end of the carriage; on the way to breakfast we'd passed him yawning contentedly whilst leaving the ransacked room and had quietly agreed to hope he wouldn't sit next to us as we pressed hurriedly on, so this positional outcome brought additional satisfaction to the day.

"How are we all this morning?" the guard asked, making his way through and looking contentedly at us all.

"Oh it's a beautiful day!" sang a response from the dancers' table along with a bout of satisfied murmurings marking agreement all round.

"You look well, you all look well!" he said, beaming around at us before continuing on down the aisles to do whatever it is he does.

It was a little later, mid-morning, that the train rolled to a halt and we discovered why the train guard might have been beaming more than usual.

"It's exercise time ladies and gentlemen!" he loudly announced.

"...WHAT?" came a unified response as the inspector tore his once-gently-rustled paper in panic.

"You can't fritter yourselves into obesity and early graves sitting around eating loud satisfying breakfasts every morn followed by wandering around banging heads on walls, can you?!" the guard replied heartily, pointing at us then out the window, "You'll run up that hill there this morning, to get you revved up for the day!"

"But I'm already revved up." D said.

"No you're not!" he snapped back to quash the little uprising.

"And are you coming on this run?" the inspector growled doubtfully at him.

"No sir, I'm to serve and protect this train, with my life!"

So mutiny-mottled muttering ensued as we started preparing mentally before actioning ourselves physically in order to transform ourselves into great runners/pioneers, donning professional gear, where possible, that might prove it.

The inspector looked hilarious. We'd met back off the train and he was in some kind of ancient exercise gear which he'd dangerously outgrown, particularly in the buttock region. Some people were giggling so he started growling and giving life-threatening stares that put an end to this childishness, and quite rightly so. Then the guard stood up on the carriage, unrolled some parchment, and started announcing stuff.

"Breakdown of route *talis est:*"

"*Talis* WHAT?" the inspector barked, looking wildly round to similarly dismayed faces.

The guard ignored this and went into rapid-fire word expulsion.

"Off train, into field, avoid cows, over wall, into field, avoid cows, over wall two, into field, avoid sheep and cows, over wall three and onto untamed land."

"Hold on hold on, how do we—"

The inspector was cut off with continued rapid fire though.

"Straight up hill, avoiding bracken and other vegetation where possible in order to minimise resistance and thereby maximising speed and energy efficiency. Upon reaching top of hill, short break in order to enjoy view and congratulate oneself. N.B. No waiting for friends to catch up in order to enjoy short chats and engage in commentary about meteorological conditions aka weather, or some view there may or may not be."

"What if we get there at the same t—"

Djako was cut off this time with a wonderfully ruthless continuation of rapid fire.

"Rapid return to cadence, of legs, full speed ahead back down the hill — no time to be wasted due to irrational or rational fear of falling — we're all in the hands of a god of kinds, be it God, nature, or an energy that we all are and always will be. After successful descent of hill at full speed, vaulting first wall using sheer momentum from rapid descent, continue at sprint to finish — back here — while leaping over walls in stylish manner for extra points."

"What are the points fo—"

And boom, D was cut clean off by continued rapid fire.

"One point for first back, one point for best leap, minus

one point for each fall, minus ten points for coming last *id est* it's not just taking part that counts."

"Wha—"

"Also, heed the bit on avoiding cows or stampede could transpire and result in death or serious injury."

The guard then rolled up his parchment in a conclusive manner as heads turned to corroborate with neighbours then gaze stricken a bit more upon the guard while processing what had just been heard.

"On my whistle!" he shouted, "GOOOOOOO!"

There was a moment of hesitation as we looked upon one another, still processing things perhaps, but then that backstabber D made a sudden and desperate break for it as he pushed and tugged his way through the throng and out towards the first wall at surprising speed. A chain reaction would follow this, and the conquest of that hill by the tracks on a morning of fresh sun and ample clinking would be attempted and remembered ever after as the *Great Ascent*. As well as the *Great Descent* which was probably even more memorable and more great due to the progressively drastic state of competitors as they clocked up trauma, both mental and physical, from the wild venturing and final breakneck speeds that were either rational or not depending on the god thing.

It wasn't long after the initial charge that I found myself alone, gently panting, climbing up a wooded slope, looking round and down to see who might be here or there chasing up the rear. But it seemed I'd be alone for now; one soul amidst the regal reign of tree and leaf and dark damp fragrant earth. So steadily thoughts came and grew to dawn another world within as the solitude caught hold, giving rise to havens fashioned for that of wild and free reflection.

And upon this reflection, I found myself wondering, and then resolving, that after all these years, my biggest loss may be that which was kind of evident, since it always stared me in the face; that which presumably stares us all in the face. Yes — love. Actually not love no, rather the loss of *faith* in love… yeah. I considered this might have been the magic in childhood; that which turned an ordinary moment into a magic one. Like the smell of fir trees, the clank of a camping cup preparing for a dose of hot choccy, or the rustle of a mother and a father who did important things out in the tent porch where monsters were held at bay. Is the dearness of these moments all just the acceptance and belief in love — a magic that connects us all to everything through some kind of consciousness. Because if not, then why were they so special, these moments of insignificance? Unless it's just innocence and ignorance, or perhaps humility even, albeit subconsciously so, when we make no claim to understand or know. Because there's all those other magic moments of inconsequence as well that need an explanation, like the sound of a guitar playing a strange Spanish tune in an old foreign town of foreign smells and sound, drifting through the bedroom window which Dad opened because it's hot, too hot to sleep, as we lie here in the night and listen with a certain longing to the sleepless town's heart beating. And the voice that comes with it which doesn't sing well, but is magic all the same; they're foreign words and what they sing of shall remain unknown, making the imagined world of each the hearer a little more alive.

And here now we do run as suddenly nostalgic fools, old aging ones who thought to know wisdom, or more than we did before. Where did the innocence of love go? The magic of love or humility, or innocence or ignorance, or whatever the hell you want to call it. Tossed away in favour of maturity, of moving on and up, of responsibility, and superiority, and ultimately, mediocrity. It was all tossed away. And so here now run a range of fools with hardly any magic left; only words and strategies, forlorn philosophies, and putting one foot in front of the other, in relatively rapid succession at times, to comfort the fear, the capitulation, the defeat that came silent one day, when love, or innocence, was tossed away.

Hmmm, maybe I'll take it back, I contemplated, *if I can find it*; so long ago, and with such neglect was it tossed away though, that I know not right now where to look. But to start looking might be a good place to begin; it might be closer than I imagined. For it knows me, I'm sure, and I it, deep down where the soul purrs.

And then I could maybe feel again... some fresh-cut grass, on a summer's day, as someone giggles not too far off perhaps, and birds chirp while a bee hums by, and then the breeze brings the light sweet smell of... some flowers I'd guess. And then of course some clown not far off — certainly not as far off as one would have liked — some miserable neighbour who's got out his loud machinery and now he's cutting through it all, this great summer's day, with inexplicable horror. And he's so *fucking* content, because his machinery seems loud and powerful and he feels more impressive now, because of the loudness and the powerfulness. But that's just how it is man. And I'd feel it how it was all meant to be felt, as one did a child, as innocence feels it, when magic runs through all. And this could be love, or faith in love — not sure which — maybe both; and I wouldn't care if we made it all up, because it's magic, and magic's all made up anyway.

CRACK!

Reality came rushing back as no other than D came into view, crashing through vision, and a rhododendron bush I'd come to find myself admiring.

"Oi…" I slowly exclaimed in surprise, "what are you doing crashing through here?"

"Lost the path," he said, "found it now — I heard people talking — but it's just you…"

I looked at him, mouth ajar a bit, but hopefully not drooling.

"Were you talking to yourself?" he continued, "And why were you staring at this bush?"

"Erm…" I said/wondered, reality still returning and not really knowing, "it's in flower isn't it, and so I was admiring it while taking a short break."

"OK…" he said, looking at me, head kind of cocked to one side, "shall we be pushing on together?"

"Hmmm," I replied as reality picked up pace again, "yeah, good idea."

So we pushed on to the top, our combined morale surely boosting us on to victory.

We reached the summit together, in the lead, and stood for a moment, back to back, so we could engage in commentary about the weather and wonderful view in quite satisfactory detail without this being evident. We proceeded to make some jokes about the stragglers hardly halfway up and then set off on our descent to precipitate ourselves rapidly back to the finish in first place where we would enjoy a wonderful spectacle in turning to watch the turmoil unfolding on the great descent behind us. The banker chugged determinedly on, slowly but surely, with such resolve that anyone would yearn for, and Enyone just walked, but at incredible speed, reminding us that these old women can be intolerably proficient at getting a task done. Witnessing the inspector rolling himself awkwardly over walls and experiencing breathing difficulty was particularly good. Meanwhile the dancers scaled walls alongside him as feathers might do in a dream, implementing acrobatic manoeuvres that were unbelievably amazing/unnecessary, lending all this scene some kind of great surrealism that left one to make note remember there might yet be some magic in our lives. And this concept of magic was only amplified when we noticed someone, yes Djako, coming down in great haste an adjacent hill, followed by an army of cows and potentially some bulls because they looked pretty big. He'd got lost and gone up the wrong hill, crossed some places he clearly shouldn't have crossed, and his blind optimism was now meeting its maker; it was a beautiful sight. So we felt some empathy for the train guard then, who sat spectating too; maybe he was quite right to send us out like this, to get us revved up for the day, to get reality firmly in check, and stir up a bit of well-needed magic. And why would he miss a chance to spectate this great spectacle, thereby denying it the viewing duty it must surely demand? So the field returned one by one to the train in varied condition, and we did some clapping and spoke some words of well done as we came together again to feel something good; something about achievement, or triumph, or just about being home again without a man down, basking in the sun of this dying morning that had surprised itself and afforded us an afternoon where we could feel good, content, and cosy for a while, because we'd done a thing.

The afternoon was passed licking wounds, caressing bruised minds, and contentedly lazing around, accompanied by a range of murmurings — some of uncertainty as to what had just happened, and some of surprised content — all in conjunction with a fair bit of confused eyebrow raising as sentiments were shared meekly between ourselves. Desire for the arrival of evening hours was notable though, when we might leave this confusing swirl of contemplation behind us in the cold light of day where the mind sits too powerful and brooding, and when a drink might be taken without an ebb of guilt for having started earlier than was approved of by people or just oneself.

Well the evening hours did come, in good time, and with a drink or some small apero taken confidently in hand, wounds needed licking no more, limbs were just limbs, and mixed murmurings had transformed into chucklings of story-tellers and story-tellees, as the Great Ascent/Descent was recounted in an array of formats and from as many perspectives as there were tellers. At one point the guard told the inspector that his punishment for last position was no alcohol that evening but as a result the inspector throttled him a bit, and so we all decided in the end that it was taking part that counts after all, and winning/losing really was for the children within us whom should be under lock and key in the classroom except for short, controlled breaks for lunch and mandatory steam release. Meanwhile, we carefully noted to ourselves internally who was the best and worst as an alternative more mature categorisation/rationalisation strategy.

It was later that evening after dinner had been enjoyed and the last coffees were being sipped, or slurped by some, that an announcement was announced; a disturbing one. We'd been looking forward to an evening of cards, idle chatter, or something of that genre, perhaps with another mystery lurking in between the flickering of lanterns that swept with us and train through dark terrain. However, just as this sure series of events seemed tantalisingly close to realisation, this disturbing announcement inflicted a savage cessation to such fantasy.

"You'll be giving your performances after dinner." the guard announced amidst surprised murmuring from some while others such as the dancers and a squawky woman seemed to gasp with pleasure.

"What?" the inspector barked, "What performances?"

"You were told to prepare some kind of artistic performance not long ago, for entertainment night tonight."

"I thought that was a joke..." he growled back.

"Errr... yeah," our table added as we raised our hands to contribute, "we thought that was a joke too."

"No joke," the guard firmly said, "and it's compulsory — check ticket terms and conditions."

I started feeling pretty flustered and upon checking with each other we agreed we were all feeling pretty flustered, Djako, D, and I. So enlisting the banker in the hope he might bring some conviction to the table, we went on to decide our performance could be more of a lesson in fire building where we'd attempt to light a controlled fire with minimal modern fire-lighting technology, and damp firewood.

"But what if people aren't interested in fire building?" the banker had worriedly agitated.

But we explained everyone liked fire building because it was human nature. Unfortunately though, before we'd hardly started, our performance got shut down as apparently fires weren't allowed inside the train, and even more unfortunately so — a real shame actually because pretty childish — certain audience members had been booing us from the start at regular intervals which diminished morale and ability to perform well. Really disappointing ambiance.

"I must say, it was disappointing and rather discouraging to be booed mid-performance," the banker dared venture to the crowd as we were shuffled off stage back to our seats, "not to mention getting shut down by the authorities on top of that."

He pushed his glasses up his nose in a disapprobatory manner as he took his seat. No one really answered though; just the odd cough and murmur came floating from the crowd as the next performance was eagerly awaited and memories of the last were gladly shunned.

The inspector's performance was actually pretty good — he recounted confidential old cases under the flicker of candlelight, and it was all really mysterious and scary. And we were forlorn for how we hadn't enlisted this great man instead of that banker idiot.

The dancers' performance was obviously really good as well — it was given without mercy to any bitter onlooker who might have been hoping to see their own suffering shared.

Then came the squawky woman who announced she'd be performing a series of dramatic readings before which she continued to perform a series of dramatic readings. Big cheers that accompany the end of performances, plays, and things of this nature, are very convenient as it's not clear, and no one need specify, whether the cheer is an acknowledgement of a riveting performance or whether it's a triumphant expression of relief that erupts when you realise you can go now and do things you always dreamt of; like playing cards, degenerating into idle chatter, or just falling asleep without being poked on an ongoing basis by a fervent adjoining spectator who didn't want you to escape persistent things by way of unconsciousness. So when she finished, we all gave a very big cheer, and with some scuffling, shuffling, and some overdue retreating, we achieved the great and calling calm of bed.

Upon regaining consciousness the next day, I found myself succumbed to a hopeless sense of dread, and wondered how the clinking and the clattering of a breakfast that was light-hearted and adorned by freshly-buttered toast and sugar cubes both brown and white, along with arrays of other redundant little delights, could ever have been endured optimistically with free will. Nothing seemed to have changed since the day before, and so the newly emerged mental situation was annoying as it was unexplained. Things now donned a shadow that hollowed, and so the future, both imminent and far, was but a weight pushing down on all the little defences mind and body could muster; only one little rampart need falter and topple, and the rest would surely come crashing down to be consumed. All things good surely were only a vulnerability or some target; more innocents that we're charged to nourish and protect, now and till the end with no respite. Well how long can one hold up what's good before what's not comes seek out what's weak to work it against all its will until its breaking and shattering, or just to its slow sagging until no form is left and only a nothingness that exhaustion hollowed out remains?

So bed seemed the safest place that day, the only place one could keep ones sanity, or continue to lose it in a calm manner. I pulled the duvet up around my shoulders so only my head could feel the nagging expectation of the outside air. The pillow was soft and made no complaints, and so tucked in like a bug in a rug as it was when the kingdom of childhood had ruled the world, I happily surrendered to sleep and dreams where if dread and darkness ever came, one could always wake up and think to know them no more.

Some more days and nights passed on this train that wouldn't stop. And relentlessness seemed obvious now; a clearness had come to be apparent, as just as this train was relentless, we surely were too, for not stopping with it. You could feel each of our selves shimmering through more one day and then fading a little the next, but always harbouring the same one we unknowingly, relentlessly imagined ourselves to be.

For Djako was sometimes quieter, sometimes louder, and sometimes tears seemed close, but always a sense of optimism was about him. And this was envied, involuntarily, because though we're told optimism is good, how can we knowingly suffer while waiting till the inevitable end, and yet embody optimism without embodying falseness too? Meanwhile, D smiled one day and perhaps dreamt the next, but always an emptiness could not escape him as he aligned so close to a bare truth. And this was envied begrudgingly, because a truth is pure but neither here nor there. And the banker was so resolved, even when all seemed unresolved. And this was envied too because who doesn't want resolve even when resolve makes no sense? Then the others were the others in their own ways which were fine ways, as were all our ways, including one that was mine, I hoped. So we were the relentless in this way, and in this fashion we pushed on, with this train that could sum us all up without too much consideration or great batting of an eye, as some people on itself.

6

THE TRAIN WAS still when I woke one morning later, and by the silence but for the muffled song of bird, and dull light that lingered outside, I guessed the sun had hardly risen. The energy felt good, possibly a result of positive thinking as opposed to negative, and so I creaked out of bed and sidled to the window to see what might be greeting us in this place that harboured welcome.

The opening of window gave rise to an air that was fresh and thin and breathed life, to a happy gurgling of water, and to a bird song that would no longer stand to be muffled. Further scrutiny revealed a hopeful stream trickling alongside us, sparkling and basking in the early morning sun, and seducing not just the ear but the eye and mind too; in fact the whole body drew to it, for unapparent reasons. It babbled down a rich valley wrapped in meadows that nurtured little flowers of such vibrant colour, great firs of stamina, and quaint grassy clearings here and there. And these lazy occupants that enjoyed the patter of rabbit foot and buzz of summer flying things, spread up the gentle valley sides into more serious, less cosy slopes above. So this was a good valley, and we were high in mountain land.

"We should go search for gold!" Djako exclaimed behind me, his consciousness/words seeming to slightly dim this bright morning.

"That's ridiculous." I replied irritably as it felt like he was ruining the moment.

Djako didn't seem to hear though, and before too long, we were all paddling about in this pure innocent stream, assaulting it with makeshift sieves, having been subjected to a series of loudly recounted great tales of prospecting and wild heroics in the Americas over breakfast. This propaganda had got people excited and so one thing had led to another.

Lunch came with mumblings and grumblings and heels that dragged as gold had proved lacking in all but those great tales that seemed less great now. What's more, feet were cold, socks were sodden, and boots would surely take a day or two, or even three or more, to dry and be in serious shape for venture once again. Yes a disappointing three or more it would surely be for those of us unfortunate enough to forget to lay them out in optimal drying conditions; and between murmurs it was agreed this misfortune would hopefully befall the teller of tales who wasn't telling so many anymore.

"Hohooo," the train guard chuckled happily, "come now — nothing that a good hearty lunch can't remedy!"

Giving his hands a delighted rub as we filed back onboard, he called out and gave a whistle.

"ONWAAARDS!"

And the train moved on, leaving this innocent place to regenerate and rejuvenate from the subjugation of mind.

With night falling that evening and refuge taken in the bar carriage, the train came to stop again, and we mulled what might await us next as we peered out through the gloom. As the creaks of halting carriages gently settled down, an eerie stillness reigned a time before slow and steady, only faint at first, we heard a crunching sound come to break the silent air, and we determined that it crept towards us, ever positively closer.

"What is it?" someone called, their tries at casual questioning boldly trying to mask a fear.

But it was too late; fear had spread throughout, already laying siege, and hounding even slightly braver men as the crunching failed to falter. And there it appeared, through the nervous breaths and twitching — a figure in the dim, crunching down the dark still carriages, as it was gravelly, and they must have been wearing thick boots. As the figure drew nearer, a face came to glow in the shadows of their lantern-light, like an orange in a cupboard or another low-lit place. And we regarded, quite collectively, this someone as they came, in trepidation, or in excited expectation, or just both of these combined. As they levelled with our window and the tension reached new bounds, they looked in through and gazed at us, seemingly one by one, before turning round without remark and trudging with apparent purpose away and through the snow. The figure steadily disappeared until we could just see their lantern-light, dying in the dim and going on to make war with darkness all alone. Until there was nothing. No word or even shuffle had dared been ventured through the moment, but I chanced a look around to find comrades that seemed frozen in this little bit of time, devoid of speech or even moderate shuffling capacity, with nothing on to grasp but this thick still unsure air.

Crrreaaaaaaachhhh…

The train groaned into action and made to move again, bringing about the breaking of the moment which was lost and time returned.

"Who the hell was that then?" Djako chuckled out.

"The train guard." someone called, as more calls and murmurs erupted throughout the carriage.

"What, really?"

"I hope not."

"Why?"

"I don't know… mutiny, degeneration of train conditions due to lack of management?"

"Yeah he doesn't really do anything…"

"Well it certainly wasn't his lantern if it wasn't the train guard," the banker remarked, "that looked like standard issue."

"How do you know about standard-issue stuff?" Djako quickly turned to ask him, *and with a hint of jealousy*, I noted to myself.

"Bloody thief." the inspector growled.

"I wonder where he went though?" I asked.

"Sleepwalking?" D proposed, "Toilet due to complications?"

"Could be foraging for stuff?" Djako suggested as D's levity was waylaid.

"In these barren forests?" the banker rightly pointed out.

"Yeah," I added, "you'd need a garden of Eden or some kind of advanced horticulture with greenhouses and things like that."

"Well we're pushing onwards now," the inspector growled on as we picked up speed and took into the night, "no time for stragglers and renegades."

And the violinist began to play in his curious melancholic way, like lost in dream, like only he possessed this train, and like he'd played and possessed this train since as far as he remembered. And as the train rolled on, sweeping through dark broken grasslands and lost valleys, it seemed time still had not redressed itself just yet — one moment slowly drawing out and sound left far behind, or maybe far in front, as the barman swivelled fine glasses in well-practised fingers that were certain of themselves, fellow passengers around us laughed, lit a cigar, or took a sip of something, and all the while they seemed to smile like they knew a thing we didn't. But maybe it was each the same for every one of us who did endure this long and feigning instant. And the beating of the train pulsed relentlessly on while the violinist played perfectly between it, both indifferent it seemed, immune to questioning and qualms of what could be classed as such a paltry passing moment. *What was going on, and had we just lost our shepherd/authoritative body aka the train guard,* we found we had to wonder as the train sped firmly forward into snow and night and pine.

I decided to return to my book then, as a defence against the disconcerting goings-on — one I'd been leaving to dust in a corner designed for such things, but reminding myself that reading material on a train really shouldn't go overlooked, I'd snatched it up as it caught my eye on the day of departure. I wasn't convinced I was enjoying it, and it was becoming apparent that it contained concepts I didn't understand or wasn't familiar with, which made me wonder whether these concepts really existed in the first place. But on balance, it seemed a relatively OK activity since good alternatives were proving scarce, *and maybe not just due to current train-bound limitations,* I dejectedly reflected. But this was probably a darker reflection than it should have been. Also it's important, it seems, to have an excuse not to talk sometimes or continuously acknowledge people in long-term close-quarter environments — a concept not familiar to, or understood by certain people, I often found myself thinking in the company of Djako; or perhaps they just don't believe the concept exists and so don't have to abide by it.

So as books, low lights, and quiet chatter drew the disconcertion to a close, the cosy rocking of the train took us on a while, until we realised one by one, that our carriage yet again was still, for a dubious third time in one day, and the air distinctly changed, lending cause for one to look up from a book, or just the floor one might have been considering as a reasonable alternative.

"Yes, three times, where one more might be one too

many." the train guard sternly uttered, "But this is where we stop and take a stand — she's here, the storm — outrun her we could never have forever done so anyway."

"Errr... since when have we been outrunning a storm?" D sceptically asked, looking around inquisitively at us.

"Action stations people," the inspector grimly said, ignoring the layman's questioning and taking to his feet, "action stations."

"What are the actions stations?" someone asked.

"I think it's just an expression," the banker said, looking tentatively at the inspector, "is it?"

But he just kind of looked back at us with a grimace or something like what old inspectors tend to do.

So this storm came, to rage before us, giving some kind of beauty that flowed across the sky, and with such elegance that it almost seemed serene. But it was definitely a storm; we would not be fooled as it lit up a sky that played with darkness and non-darkness and all those colours in between because it was old and must have come to terms with things that come and go. So it greeted this storm with open arms, facilitating the smooth flow of chaos in serene fashion, to chaos' grand surprise.

And smiling too through our surprise, we sat beneath light rain atop a carriage of the train, which itself sat still and silenced, lending the little pings and tings of timid raindrops falling on it their moment of soft melody. And on this great viaduct we'd come to linger on, that sat perched between two blackened peaks rising out of reach to night and endless

sky above, we might have thought we were some rulers regarding on our kingdom, or just some people on a hill who
observed and lightly wondered. Either way, we occupied
this grand place in our defiant anoraks, with little room for
contestation, *like a regiment going to the front*, someone had
proffered, *going to death and destruction, or some glorious victory if not.* We agreed that this was a nice proposition as it
seemed heroic, and also it felt like some of us were begin-
ning to think it true.

The storm surged and swept across the unyielding land,
trying to claim that it would be uncontested too, as rumbles
rolled across to meet our heroic ears and the sky continued
to flash and crackle to light up the dark of this barren, empty
plain which didn't seem like much of a kingdom after all.
We sat in silence as we gazed, although you could hear the
odd slurp as someone took a sip of tea. But it was comforting
to hear such a noise under the current circumstances/mete-
orological conditions, as maybe it brought with it some
humanity and goodness to a distant place that would otherwise be indifferent and without consequence.

A window sliding open with an air of frustration was
heard below and one of the dancers stuck her head out.

"What are you doing out there?!" she hissed, holding
back no tone of discontent, "I can't sleep for all your slurping!"

"You should come up here," the banker called, "it's a
darn fine sight, and there's a goodness in the air tonight."

We heard the window slide shut again followed by some
muffled debate below.

"...Right, we're all going up on the roof!" someone

called, "There's a darn fine sight and a goodness in the air!"

An array of clanks and clicks, thuds and other muffled sounds could be heard in the carriage below as it awakened throughout, and shortly after, a train of shadows came clambering out, crunching on the gravel below then up the ladder to this night's auditorium that would be the carriage roof. The excited whispers and clamouring emitted by the new arrivals gradually died down as seating positions were taken up, and after a few minutes we were all out together, settled in a new and improved extended line. And the guard too, who stood watch at the end — a silhouetted figure just, but a comforting one. The banker had organised tea for everyone so the once-sporadic slurping had intensified into a slurping comparable to that of rapid machine gun fire rendering this tea a harsh warning sound to any warfare-savvy soul that might have dared prowl too close below. But this noise pollution was fine; it could be our unwavering retaliation to the great booming of a storm that could never really compete.

So we sat and sipped and awed a bit, as our storm danced and soared as it saw fit. And as its stage was lit and battered by frustration, it was nice to be above and away from it all, under the light rain as this felt like a welcome friend in comparison.

"I think it's coming our way," the inspector called, "best be readying ourselves…"

"Naaah," Djako replied confidently, "it's going across the plain — not our way."

"We could count the seconds between light and thunder." someone suggested.

So we counted the seconds between light and thunder for a while, although we found ourselves with differing results as there was disagreement over second-length and no clock could be mustered. Therefore, some customary bickering ensued and took hold of this timeless train top. But in the heat of debating second-counting technique, an undeniable tone of irresistibility came upon us so commandingly then, to interrupt the fracas that had come to unfold. And so with heads turned, battle cries fell silent, and a calm invaded this place again as the violinist was spotted, playing before the dying storm which indeed was only sweeping by across the plain, and was but purring at us now, perhaps tamed too by the lone lament of a violinist that filled the air with such authority, breaking boom of storm and even uncontested time that had ruled this place too long.

"Where is he!? Where is he?!" hushed whispers hissed between us.

"There!" the inspector bellowed, pointing in excitement, "There out on the precipice!"

And there he was, joined by the two dancers, dancing on the precipice alongside him, in the moonlight by now that lit them up like some kind of spirits that might not have been there at all. So some degree of mesmerisation ensued as we sipped our tea, ate our oranges (the train guard had distributed oranges by this point), and gazed even more so than before as these fantoms played and danced like it was the last night or the first and only night they might exist.

"Wow, these oranges are excellent!" the banker called, "From where do they hail?"

"I picked them up a little while back." the train guard

answered happily.

"Oh," someone called over, "so that was you getting off the train and crunching along the gravel with a lantern?"

"Ohohoo yes," he chuckled, pointing round at us with an ending linger on the inspector, "even for slightly braver men, dark oranges in cupboards may be fearsome!"

"Bahhh, how did you catch up with us then?" the inspector snapped to wave off the lingering finger and curious eyes it drew towards him, "We've been going at what must have been high speed for ages since then!"

"You've just done a big loop son — I walked between the two sections of track and rejoined the train here."

"...So he must have been listening to us talking after," D softly mused, "the bit about him looking like an orange in a dark cupboard, because that's no standard-issue expression."

"Yeah," I remarked a little surprised myself as I looked over at the guard in what felt like fascination, "and he's used it back on us with insincerity..."

There followed a short interlude as the inspector did some standard-issue ranting and we reflected for a while about route choice and where we were even going etc., before we quite rightly got back to the moment in question.

"Why are you speaking like that?" D asked the banker.

"Like what?"

"Using words like *hail*."

"Well... I-I'm—"

"He's excited lad," the inspector chuckled giving the banker a pat on the back, "let him speak as he'll speak!"

"I wonder if he knew this storm was coming," Djako suggested, "and he picked the oranges specially?"

"What," I said, "like a kind of popcorn you mean?"

"Yeah, like a kind of popcorn…"

"Go get some more oranges!" the inspector barked.

"…And more tea!" the banker added, before murmurs of content agreement resounded up and down the carriage top.

And I thought these were good ideas too as I took another sip of tea and smelt the tangy perfume of an orange that rolled in hand while marvelling about the combination of hot tea and fresh oranges consumed under such conditions.

"What a nice combination of things." I said out loud.

"What?" D demanded.

"He means the tangy oranges," Djako interjected, "the hot tea, the view across the plain, and all these other things that've been unfurling under the exceptional conditions."

And I had to give it to this clown, because he'd spoken it all true.

7

THE NEXT MORNING brought us steaming through glen and wildland that nurtured swathes of barren moor rolling down from left and right. And alongside us, reigning the middle of the glen, a great lake stretched out and sparkled in the fresh pale morning sun, home to jumping fish, far-reaching shores, and some gliding hunting bird that would sometimes graze the surface to ally at leisure with wind and water, making us and our train look cumbersome and ill-conceived, yet all the more relentless for we pushed on nonetheless. Drifting off in bed the night before to thundery echoes of a dying storm passing away to another place seemed like a world away now; and it all felt good, this new world and this memory of the last, as one day we might miss it all and perhaps feel a twang of longing that reminds us for what we live for.

So it was another optimistic morning and breakfast was

passed in relative cheeriness where rustle of newspaper and bustle of breakfasty things was emitted and received with ease and satisfaction. And this optimistic start would develop into a lazy mid-morning where we'd read a bit and talk a little, while some would write or window gaze, and one or two would stroll down train and up, to look au fait and feel of certain use. And because this was a lazy day with an optimistic start, no demand was present; no itching gnawing sense that we should be doing something more, or thinking something more, was hanging overhead. So we could enjoy this laziness as it deserved to be enjoyed rather than fighting it like an American or something else that lacks finesse and self-restraint.

But perhaps inevitably, before long, as the lake stretched on and on, questioning was bound to triumph and bring fraught fretting back to trouble mind again; *what deep depths this great lake must possess?* Look at it lapping silently at its bounds — did it lap with no sense of hunger as man might lap at his? And look, that bird soars above still, boasting pristine wings and such a royal confidence that simply seems to beam, to dazzle any onlooker as she sweeps as high or low as she might please, sometimes so low to gently brush the icy water, to become one for a time and ignite something we might not see — set in motion something we maybe cannot see, and would probably never see for it's not for us to perceive, beyond all realms of the perception of man.

I thought I might like my mind to be like this lake; all silent and deep, and all embracing to such disturbances as the talon of a bird or splash of some fish. But while the lake shimmered in tranquil glory at first, as we passed along its lengths, something darkened and grew too ominous for that of confidence; tranquillity proved transient without real depth or stamina, and another force showed itself to be seeping through the surface. The lake seemed to groan — what for, we could only hazard a guess. For the weight of ten thousand years, or ten thousand more to come? For some release from this bounded prison between the rock it had known too long now? Or was it us that made it groan, was it groaning at us — at the man who murmured and scribbled until contented in the corner; at our questioning that would not cease; or at perhaps the general spewing of sound from mouths which claimed to know. So we sat and felt uneasy as we considered this new complex and felt more vulnerable than before, our hearty breakfast but a fading notion now, like so many other old and obsoleted ones.

And this great expanse that would not stop to run beside us, teasing all along, teased yet more questions that came from the shallows of our tracks; we could not precise what love is, what meaning was, or indeed who we might be — what *what* would be. Perhaps this makes the moment worth it, each moment worth it; was this imprecision what made each moment worth it? As did this lake, or this bird fret on mapping out love or meaning or any other great-seeming thing? No surely not, but of course not; they don't speak words; they do not care for squiggles and sounds that we might emit to realise and to categorise, and to rationalise things that should never really be *-ised* for that's not what they were made for. No, they are at peace with the imperceptible; that which words only corrupt and pollute; that which is bound by no word. They saw not the world through a disjointed layer of map backed by made-up sounds and numbers, categories and definitions, and hopeful other things; it must have been more fluid for them, more satisfactorily one. And maybe they knew an essence that our layers of map had come to smother. For if all these concepts, be them normative or physical, abstract or whatever kind of other philosophical, are either make-believe or infinite, then potential to map, and to perceive yet more, is surely endless. So through our pursuing of perception backed by our poor disjointed mapping, this continued reliance on our ability to perceive and -ise may only lend ourselves to lostness time and time again, for the infinite was never findable. And so there lied some truth maybe, that which we all might seek, out there away upon the lake where reigned the inconceiving, or perhaps just the undesiring, mind of a peaceful moment.

While perhaps hours passed, but maybe days, or possibly weeks or more — either way it probably doesn't matter — the haziness of things progressed and persevered, and it all just could have been a dream, when true consciousness, allegedly, seemed to take a worthy stand, and envelop is in peace, or something not quite tangible but nice and warming nonetheless. And life was pretty good a while.

Though before too long, like some ancient shielding spell was lifted, in the blinking of an eye too quick for any one of us to notice, we awoke from this welcome subjugation, to conceive, and resume realising things that were probably not true. So until dominion over the erring mind would at last become afoot for sure and in a suitably consistent manner, our layered veil comprising contestable pieces of map through which truths must surely pass corrupted, would not be lifted. But more important matters were at hand now; easier and more realisable ones that didn't gnaw as much, though actually that kind of did, because they were just difficult in a different kind of way.

"Such is the nature of time." we found the banker saying.

"Ha, what do you know of time!" D laughed back.

"Oh and what do you know of anything, you miserable man!"

"I know about the minor key, and major too; fine wine, may that be red or white, decanted in the midst of a belle so starry soirée; the swift fall of aging empire; har—"

"What?" I interrupted.

"What?" he said.

"What's this about aging empires?"

"Oh I studied ancient history a while."

"Oh… and what about the fine wine thing?"

"I thought that just sounded good."

"OK. And so the history thing's true though?"

"Yeah, yeh, I studied it a few years I think, yeah pretty sure it was at least one, with a few breaks… yeah… there was a few breaks."

I just looked back at him for a bit, words failing me be it my fault or his, and then out the window instead because it was easier. But I was still wondering whether to bear ask him about the minor-major key thing as well, so couldn't really concentrate on nice stuff like the view etc.

And meanwhile the man in the corner squiggled on while those in the carriage chattered on, and we were none the wiser for they, after all, were just squiggles and sounds, from tired old tongue or hand, that knew too many bounds to give passage to some incorruptible or great truth. And *click* went the little blind that knocked against the window as the train rocked on and we gazed on at this great lake that flowed on with bird and fish and perfectly balanced moments, and whatever other damn things were lurking there. And *tappedy click tap CLICK* went the damn little blind.

"I wonder if it's windy out?" someone called across the carriage as we window-gazed en masse.

We could not know for sure, since we were not without, only within as we pushed on along these silent shores. But the water was still, ever so still, which begged one to wager no wind blew. Though then again, this water was unnaturally still, too still to warrant lack of question; yes, a trick of the eye was at work here we alleged — we were certain of it now — and the silent stealthy wind which surely blew would not deceive us this time, we thought together as we rubbed our hands in victory and smiled with glee at one another.

"More tea!" the inspector called over to the barman, "More tea! This wind's rusing has been scuppered!"

Then turning back to us, and again looking from one to another, we continued to exchange devious smiles and slurp excessively in order to enjoy our basking in triumph and the extended tea break we'd undoubtedly earned this morning after all our clever reckonings.

"...It's weird for such a big lake to not even have a single ripple," the banker remarked as the rubbing of hands subsided, "is that even possible, be it windy or not?"

There followed a short pause as we reflected.

"...Go get the mathematician." the inspector said, half-sighing, and nodding over to the corner where he sat and scribbled.

After prolonged discussion which followed the mathematician's comments on the matter, we decided we were perhaps too far away to see whether there were really any ripples or not — they could just be small ones the mathematician had pointed out, and so we might just not be perceiving them.

"So the wind wasn't trying to deceive us after all?" the banker softly uttered, "Just gently blowing and giving rise to lazy ripples we did not see?"

But only blank faces and glassy-eyed stares answered back, as teas went cold, and next cups would have to wait a while before they could be enjoyed anew once we'd forgot about the pleasure of the last.

In a flash the lake ended, proving itself not so great, and the delirium was done; the spell of the infinite, amongst other things, lifted in the nick of time as we felt ourselves return to sanity/reality. We froze for a moment though and looked — half full of hope, half full of fear for some ghastly relapse back to questioning and trappings of lakes and the infinite amongst other things — as the train guard came and made to speak.

"Right." he said with an inhabitual curtness that accompanied a dishevelled hue come to taint his cheerful manner, "…That's lunch."

We pulled into a little platform soon after and placated a while there a small clearing in the woods. A little lane ran up to this seemingly forgotten place that even maps might not know, and we wondered what might roam to greet us here, or who might dare to disembark from the safety of the train to find out. It was a fine place, full of bird song and easily overcoming any human attempt to interfere through twiddling and taming and naming. So we were glad to find out lunch would be savoured here, served out on the green grass in the thick of it all, which actually looked a bit tamed because it was short and neat, and must have been mown. There followed a standard hustle and bustle of excited murmuring and scuffling as this news of imminent lunching came to light, and we all disembarked to find a makeshift restaurant upon the grass all ready to receive, with little round tables and white tablecloths and a couple of waiters here and there with gloves and towels hanging over arms which made them look important and made us feel so too.

On one table there were some foreign faces looking pleased with themselves, perhaps with the knowledge that they'd secured their seating positions of choice before anyone else had had the chance to choose theirs, and so they were eyed with a degree of suspicion. One spoke quite unseemly, in a muffled manner, like he had a cold or something, so he'd be edged away from and softly shunned each time he'd draw to speak, to minimise viral discharge. And the other looked slightly fed up, like he wasn't drinking as much wine as he'd have liked. We decided to sit at the table next to them for lunch — Djako, D, and I — as all the other tables had been quickly occupied and we were exposed to be the less experienced restaurant-goers amongst us.

"But it's a similar concept to finding and occupying seats on a train," I murmured disappointedly to Djako and D as we took up our dining positions, "so we could have successfully reapplied it here."

"But it was a lazy morning and we were caught off guard." Djako consoled, even as he too looked dampened in spirit.

We chose to keep our spirits up though and engaged with these newcomers as best we could, kicking things off by asking what they were doing here. They claimed to be reviewing restaurants or something.

"Careful with that please!" one of them jittered as his rucksack was taken from the chair he'd rested it upon in order to clear space for more appropriate use.

"What's the problem?" D asked.

"This bag is a state-of-the-art receptacle," he replied with impressive conviction, "designed to withstand extreme cold, high intensity precipitation, and I'm told, even in beachhead environments, sand would struggle to penetrate the protective membrane. Yes, you might say this rucky flirts with the limits of invincibility itself."

"Right, so why do I need to be careful with it?"

"I... was told nothing of its resistance to wine staining

and would like to preserve its aesthetic."

"Why do you need such a hi-tech piece of equipment for reviewing restaurants and conservatively drinking wine anyway?" Djako noted, surprisingly sensibly.

The man mused, building a surprisingly enjoyable anticipation before he spoke.

"That's... just the kind of guy I am." he replied, smiling wryly to himself as the muse still left its mark along with the audacious response.

"Oh wow." D remarked as the man looked triumphantly at us.

But he went on to mention some interesting stuff along the lines of how we should look forward to failure so courage to reach for that which is desired might be more easily mustered, be it folly or not, permitting satisfaction in having reached at least, regardless how it all turned out. I was liking it, I was liking it a lot; the principle felt, at the time, like it must entail ultimate liberation, particularly perhaps if you were to consider one's final breath a failure.

So, to mixed emotions, they said goodbye after lunch, presumably wandering on to a next restaurant to carry on the important work. We watched them drift off down the little lane that disappeared into the woods.

"So this place must be known by some," D said, "I wonder how they got here?"

"Special contacts?" Djako proposed.

"Secret documents slash maps?" I added.

"Hmmm..." D responded in thought.

"Or maybe they're just... stumbling around aimlessly and they happened upon this place?" I suggested, "That rucksack could hold weeks of supplies."

"Maybe they're ghosts — dead men..." Djako said in a hushed tone to bring a close to the debate which I'd now moved on from, since debating whether I might start calling it a *rucky* too, particularly when feeling raucous, had become pressing, "...they seemed sinister enough."

The train took us on after lunch, to leave the cosy little clearing in the woods behind and slice through new horizons. And sure enough, it wasn't long later that a whole new entity was spotted; that which a mouldy old lake could never compete with, however great or infinite. The sea came into view. Only small and distant at first, but undoubtedly the sea. Unless it was just some more sky or low funny-coloured cloud. But no, it was the sea. Because we couldn't decide for a while and extended debate ensnared us all, but it *was* the sea, because we eventually got there, and then no one could debate anymore since it was clearly there at last. We'd come to find ourselves atop an old forgotten fjord where maybe some Vikings used to sail ships, or take a romantic cliff-walk perhaps and admire the view; in the snow and ice sometimes, but on summer mornings when rabbits played too; because presumably they did nice activities like that when they weren't raiding and stuff, although this became a new topic of debate for a time because we weren't sure. There was of course some customary *oohing* and *aahing* when the sea was at last formally identified and spotted with a higher degree of confidence, and we all felt obliged to join in while privately enjoying the redundant spectacle because it made us feel young again and innocent.

"Look!" one of the dancers called, "The sea!"

And we all rushed to the window to awe and gape in excited soft murmur while some would choose to point, to really make sure, that it was there before us now, nonchalantly glinting in the sun and marshalling an endless stage for where each day could rise or set, depending on angles.

"Here we are people!" the train guard called, "The end of the line for now!"

But what will we do? and other hushed frantic whisperings scurried through the tantalising atmosphere that came to take the carriage now.

"There's a boat will take you over to the other side — me and these carriages need another break from delirium and drivel — we're going around for some well-earned maintenance and repairs."

"Well how long till the boat?" someone rightly shouted out, "What supplies do we need?"

"Yeah, and the other side of what?" the banker added, "Are we talking about that deep and dark-looking fjord?"

"There it is!" the guard called as he pointed down below us to a suspiciously steep looking cliff, "Everybody off! Everybody off! Leaves in... twenty minutes!"

So we were scrambled off in haste, like irregularly stirred egg, leading to lack of smoothness, mayhem, and mutterings of malcontent; the recent excitement of sea-spotting all whisked away and turned to wisps of memory.

Djako and I found ourselves leading the way once more, as we had done all that time ago when we'd tackled the old hotel. *The Boat*, read the little signpost that directed us out of the rocky platform cut direct into the hillside. So we decided to follow without much need for question or corroboration. The path was small and treacherous, and mighty steep down the fjord side that dropped into the sea below, to where the lonely boat supposedly awaited. As expected, most of us had inappropriate footwear due to lack of prior information supplied by the authorities, while high-speed train evacuation had lent little time for external observation and planning. We also had to carry our baggage for the un-expected expedition, and some had elected to take whole suitcases containing different styles and colours of garment etc., you know, just in case. So this picturesque way down to the little cove below was plagued by cursing and injury, and damaged suitcases, some of which were made by peo-ple with important names which made the damage even more unacceptable. But, well, it turned out we'd had some training not so long ago, in rapid steep downhill descents, and so with particularly wry smiles all round we knew vic-tory would be ours this day, like a band of fearsome Vikings might have had against… another band of slightly less fear-some Vikings on this cliff one time when they weren't doing nicer alternatives like the romantic cliff stuff.

"I don't believe this!" the inspector growled as he slipped and tripped his way down, his suitcase presently stuck be-tween the rocks.

"Well," Enyone tutted at him, "what *do* you believe in, hmmm?"

"Crime and the delicate art of deduction!"

"Ha!" D laughed, "But you're useless at deduction!"

"Come here you little punk!"

"What about numbers?" the banker interrupted, "Who believes in them?"

"Just another human invention." someone called from behind.

"WHAT!?" the inspector blurted out, "Where's the mathematician?"

"He's down in front." one of the dancers called up from below.

"Right, get a message to him: *do numbers exist or not?*"

The message was passed down the descending line and we waited in anticipation.

"He says he uses them as a tool to help rationalise the world." the message came back.

"Well he hasn't said if they exist or not." the banker pointed out.

"Yeah, the priest would say the same about God." D said, "Ask the priest if he'd say the same about God."

"Where's the priest?" the inspector barked.

"He's behind, up above." the other dancer called, struggling down just behind us, cases with names now impeding any unnecessary feather-like manoeuvres.

"Right, get the message to him."

And the message was passed up the line while we waited again in anticipation.

"He says God helps him understand the world." the message came back.

"Right..." the inspector demanded, "is that the same as what the mathematician said about numbers?"

"Think it might be." D said.

"So does that mean they exist or not?" the banker queried.

"Look!" Djako cried, "How can numbers not exist — those trees there — one, two, three!"

"Those trees there," D said, "God, God, God."

We endured a short pause as people thought.

"…Get another message to the mathematician!" the inspector growled.

And so on went more exchanges that were shouted and circulated and corrupted along the way as they passed up and down the descending line. Plus I had a nasty suspicion that the dancers weren't taking it seriously and were intentionally tampering with the original messages as they were transmitted. So confused debate unfurled a while as we struggled on down.

"The problem is," the artist called from up above, "as soon as we give something characteristics — God, or whatever you might call it — we've corrupted it and made it into something that doesn't exist, since we imagined it."

"So we should be believing in something what we don't know what it is?" Djako determined.

"Yeah!" the banker cried, "Cut the know-it-all stuff out and it might just be something worth believing in!"

"Right," someone shouted up from down below, "so what we're saying is we should be believing in something we can't perceive, yet we presume does indeed exist and is something good?"

"Hmmm, what's good though?" D shouted back down, "Could be bad for some and good for others?"

"OK yeah, erm, something worth living for?" they

shouted back up.

"What, like the end of this relentless journey?" D muttered.

"Perhaps exactly that." the banker tutted at him.

"Or..." Djako started, chuckling to himself and looking round at people, "this so-called boat, I mean, where is it!? Maybe this so-called boat doesn't exist either and he's sent us on a wild goose chase, and it's—"

The boat appeared then, as we turned a final corner, and I smiled gladly to myself while contemplating Djako's face, and also while still enjoying the believing in something we can't perceive thing.

So our short-term destiny was fulfilled as we came to the boat, which was waiting for us all quite leisurely in its little port with naught but a small box of a ticket office which looked weather-worn and wise, and it made us think of mysteries and memories and things that might have happened long ago when things were surely simpler.

8

DJAKO AND I SAT in the bar of the boat which enjoyed panoramic views of the fjord we followed. No one else was there yet and so we savoured the moment alone while discussing the characteristics of the boat such as bedrooms, corridors, window size and frequency, etc.

"It's basically the same as being on the train but a bit wider." Djako was saying.

I disagreed and went on to explain how the whole motion of a train was different to that of the boat, and the ambiance nothing alike, leading to a completely different transportation experience.

"Mmm, nah, it's basically the same as being on the train but a bit wider." he repeated as if he hadn't already just said it, and this was frustrating.

So I decided to just repeat what I'd said as well.

"No, the whole motion of a train is different to the boat

and the ambiance nothing alike," I said whilst watching for what he would do, "leading to a completely different transportation experience."

But he just looked out the window as if everything was normal. And we continued a while in this vein as we crept up the fjord and as mountains came to sharply rise on either side, entrusting a dark corridor of deep water to guide us to a place we hoped was good.

After discussions about the boat came to an end and we couldn't think of anything else to talk about, we decided we should look for dolphins or some other exciting sea creature that might happen upon and welcomely disturb the surface of this otherwise disappointingly uniform water. Well we watched for about an hour and didn't see anything so decided we probably shouldn't look for dolphins or any other sea creature again. A few moments later the banker and D came bursting in to disturb the otherwise uniformly dull atmosphere.

"Hahaaa! What a sight!" the banker was crying, "Dolphins, whales, and all kinds of other exciting sea creatures, making glorious this lonely silent sea!"

We pretended not to be very interested and asked if they wanted a drink. It was apparent though that Djako wasn't recovering very well.

"So where did you see these creatures?" he asked in his best nonchalant attitude.

"Just off the back of the boat," the banker chuckled, "only an idiot would have been looking out the front!"

Djako and I glanced at each other again, feeling increasingly perturbed.

"Yeah, I've seen loads of whales and stuff like that before," I said, "but well done there."

"So have *you* been looking for dolphins and things?" D asked, looking at us suspiciously and seeming to suspect something.

"Nahhh — no," I quickly replied, "we were just discussing politics and things like that... because yeah, I've seen loads of whales and stuff like that before."

"Nice." Djako said aloud, even though it should have been an in-head reflection only.

"What's nice?" D quickly countered.

"You know, the politics and things." I said as Djako flailed for assistance.

"Riiight..." he chuckled back as he knocked on the bar for some service.

It had steadily become apparent that D was annoyingly intuitive. But at least the others could always believe heroes and great men existed amongst us.

"So have you got a girlfriend?" Djako asked the banker a while later when we'd taken up position in some comfy chairs not too far from the bar and offering prime panoramas of our way forward through the fjord.

"Yes, wife, longtime married," he replied in a wonderfully proud and serious manner, "woman of my life — any word against her and I will destroy you."

"Lovely stuff." the inspector remarked with a spirited grin as he passed hastily by cradling his whisky and paper.

"Confidence in a relationship," D continued, "what an excellent rarity, yeah, love is easy, but conviction and confidence..."

"Yeah," I agreed, "I'd have a bit of that if I could get my hands on it."

"Confidence and conviction chaps," the banker chirped, "it's not partial differential equations."

"Yeah, or whale watching…" D added, giving Djako and I an unnecessary look.

"Well I have confidence and conviction in my relationships." Djako said confidently and loudly, perhaps to make his sentence seem more true.

"But from what you've told us your relationships always quickly end," I remarked, "and usually not well."

"Yes, note well," the banker said through pursed lips as he gave Djako a disapproving regard, "there's a fine line between C and C and blind idiocy slash optimism."

"What's C and C?" D asked as we looked to the banker questioningly.

"Confidence and conviction."

"O yeah…" we chorused back.

"…So how do we tell which side of the line we're on?" I questioned after a short pause.

"You just have to wait and see," the banker continued, "with a bit of luck you'll be on the right side."

"OK," we cheered as we clinked glasses and pushed on with things, "here's to a bit of luck!"

As we mingled and muttered on into the evening and discussions originating from the descent down to the boat resumed themselves, it turned out that the dancers had indeed been messing with the original messages as no one seemed to be able to agree on what was originally said or eventually concluded, though there were those who suggested wilful sabotage might not be the only possible offender. So due to even more confusion developing, we decided to just believe in what we originally believed and leave it at that for now. Then we could move on to more pressing subjects like fire building, and what drinks should be served with ice, water, or nothing at all. But we didn't really arrive at any concrete conclusions here either, plus some people complained that we'd already discussed certain subjects numerous times before and that they weren't very exciting the first time.

So did the boat push bravely on along as night fell across our darkening corridor. And with lamps lit, some kind of swing band appearing, drinks poured, and in dynamic company as the dancers had decided to join us for dinner giving way to some moderate courting and plenty of *josh* as Djako kept referring to it, we were ready to weather the night with this little boat.

"Happiness is not pertinent," D barked out as the evening effervesced, "desire is that which must be pursued, without cease, knowing that our one true desire may only be to pursue desire, leading to the unsatisfactory conclusion that in achieving our desires, there will be no ultimate satisfaction, as our one true desire remains unmoved, as it was always timeless."

I found myself feeling like this sounded suspiciously like something I'd said before about destiny and mountain climbing, although somehow rephrased to sound different. I couldn't really prove it though, and these people probably didn't remember anyway. So I looked at D with some degree of anger, though not in such evidence that other people might notice, because I didn't want to look like I was losing my cool. And meanwhile I wondered whether he was taking his *to be confirmed* revenge from all that time ago back at that hotel.

"How long did it take you to think that up?" I asked.

"Just improvved it right now." he replied nonchalantly as he won a few more wows from the crowd.

What a liar, I thought, although I couldn't be certain, and again it couldn't be proven, so the anger increased. I thought then I'd take my revenge at a later date, to be confirmed, and tried to think of merrier things, like being away from all these imbeciles who were potentially appreciating someone else's drivel more than mine.

"I thought true desire is to be truly conscious and aware of one's self," someone then piped up through the babble of discussion, "through the decoupling and disidentification from one's mind."

But D pretended not to hear, and I was in no mood to follow up on this bait either.

"Right then in achieving that would you even have any desire anymore?" the bait-taking artist sniggered back, "must be pretty boring…"

"Naaaah, it's not about desire," the inspector growled, "it's about faith!"

"What," D replied sceptically, "to believe in some kind of junk we made up?"

"Nahhh! To have faith!" he shouted back, "To believe in something we didn't make up cos we don't know what it is!

Just the faith that it exists and it's a good thing and it's worth living for! That's what true faith is!"

"Hey that sounds like something someone said on the way down to the boat!" the banker cried accusingly.

"Yeah and so what?" the inspector barked back, "I liked it. And I'm pretty sure I always thought it anyway."

"And actually it progressed into rather more a statement about the concept of *faith*." the mathematician interjected thoughtfully, to a satisfied grunt and rough shoulder squeeze from a proudly smiling inspector.

So we continued some increasingly excitable philosophical discussions which became increasingly ill-clarified yet satisfactory as the vintage wine of the old boat cellars flew freely and the hour drew on. And it was good fun for while it lasted, until the next morning would arrive, when bright belief and rolling levity would become but pale thinking and hesitation once again.

After the night had been passed in respective cabins, again shared in my and Djako's case due to inflexible sleeping plan arrangements which were proving constant and non-negotiable across all transportation formats, we were enjoying mid-morning coffee in the common room when came an amusing offer.

"Right, who wants to sail the next stage of the fjord?" the captain announced, "Those interested, meet me on the bridge."

It seemed there weren't many takers as I chuckled to myself and peered around the room for any unfortunates who might be thinking this proposal sounded like a good idea, before sensing that Djako was standing up next to me, because everyone was staring over at us, and a shadow had come to mire my half-drunk coffee cup.

"We'll do it!" he shouted out, "I've sailed loads of times back home."

I protested a bit but actually felt a strange desire to just go and do it too; maybe I thought we'd get another chance to see all those dolphins and things, and up close too — see them properly — not like any of these other fakers; or maybe Djako's optimism was infecting me. So a short while later I found myself walking to the bridge, a mixture of confusion and anticipation playing havoc within; and again, strangely enough, a surprising confidence in Djako, who walked beside with such courage and conviction, or possibly just ignorance and blind optimism depending on which side of the line we were currently on; the banker was in our wake somewhere far behind us though, so this predicament could be, or had to be, disregarded.

The sea air, so close to the surface of the water now, brought a freshness to face and lung that almost stung, as we splashed across the gentle waves that rolled across the fjord to exact a lull on fast-paced things. And with the exhilaration that came to hand then, comparable to climbing up high mountain peaks, or running through a foggy glen, I wondered whether we really could just substitute all this with mind simulation techniques; those ones we might employ so we might not need extend ourselves to such extravagant exploration, but be back home rather after all was fared, with hardly a scratch to bear, because in body we never did leave. It had seemed like a good solution for life simplification all that time ago near journey beginnings when I'd been deliberating on the train with D, and when Djako had been laughing inappropriately. But I wondered for a second then, as the salty spray blew across my squirming face, whether maybe Djako's laughing was not so far from apt.

And then the surface of this once-disobliging water broke, alive with fins and taily things and sometimes whole damn creatures, breaking out from this sea we once dared deem, disappointingly drab and dull. The dolphins had come to join us, to splash as we did splash, and permit us feel like animal too once more as they were, freeing us from something somehow, that hung above us or just bored within us. And just as I looked at Djako in surrender perhaps, bowing before how right he was, he did a turn, or maybe just the wind picked up; I couldn't be certain as I wasn't knowledgeable about seafaring; anyway, the boom swung round and smashed me in the head. I went down, straight down screaming in anger and pain. The dolphins disappeared; they took a different turn, maybe due to noise pollution; and I was getting loads of spray in my eyes now and it was stinging and I could only wonder what a wile it had all been, this folly adventure on the sea.

So I decided to lie down in the boat for the rest of the sailing, and gaze at the sky between long bouts of eye closing in order to try and simulate being back on the big normal boat, drinking a glass of wine and looking out the window, or just lying in bed in a private cabin, because in my simulation I didn't have to share with idiots. Djako started singing then so I quickly intervened.

"What sailing experience have you got exactly?" I asked him.

"Oh I used to sail when I was young."

"Yeah, what age?"

"I'd say about... six."

"Six!" I cried out, "What, were you sailing toy boats?"

"Ohhh these little dinghy-type boats." he said, "Yeah, not toys, but I think they were for children... yeah they were for children I think."

"So why did you think it appropriate to risk it all on the open sea in a proper adult boat based on that?"

"It's like riding a bike." he said.

"Right, well next time you do a turn can you tell me in advance so the boom doesn't smash me in the head?"

"Nahhh, that was just the wind did that — nothing I could do — nature took its course."

Idiot, I thought, and wondered if what he said was true, while closing my eyes again to simulate.

We took refuge on a pebbly beach soon after and sent up a flare, because we didn't reach the agreed official pick-up point due to factors. There was someone playing a banjo or something not far off, and so we lay, at considerable distance from one another due to factors, and listened while we waited.

"Listen to that," Djako called over, while I winced and he

continued forth nonetheless, "and I challenge you try not to think about the sun; it's setting on a plain, out in the Wild West, and you've a whisky in hand. And there's a bargirl wiping down a table nearby — her breasts are on the offbeat — they're protruding — but not too much. Oh, and she smiled at you, I think? Or did she? No one can know for sure. So you just keep rolling your cigarette, and smile privately, knowing you've got this one. It's a good smile — a knowing one — it's a fine smile, and it's just for you…"

Before I knew what was happening, I was smiling privately to myself, as the dulcet droning tones of the banjo took hold of me, the gentle lapping of the sea appeased me, and his stupid story about cowboys or something got the better of me.

"…Are you smiling?" he called over.

"No." I said, quickly, but too quickly to not arouse suspicion, I thought with disappointment.

"Yerrrr was smiling." he said, chuckling to himself, and I couldn't believe how annoyed I was getting at him, with the brazen disregard for basic conjugation just taking the whole situation unbelievably far beyond the pale.

So I suggested a skimming competition where I went on to crush him, *because he doesn't know about angles and other subtle things like I do*, I thought smiling to myself. His stones just hit so hard and heavy upon the water's edge, where mine skipped like vengeful ballerinas, bounding to the front. So things were really starting to look up again, as the proper big boat came now too, into view.

As we stepped back on the boat, we enjoyed a round of applause and various words of praise; they'd already forgotten our endeavour was a failure, or they just didn't understand.

"Ohhh," we heard a dancer cooing, "the Vikings have returned!"

And this felt pretty good; maybe we *were* like Vikings; and so I enjoyed a private smile as we were corralled through to the common room, where we would tell great tales and be bestowed hot cups of tea.

I went to bed soon after dinner because I had a headache, due to factors/booms. I tried simulating not having one but it didn't work, so then I decided to actually enjoy having one, and that did work which I thought was pretty funny; it never saw that one coming. So I permitted myself another private smile, although wondered whether that was getting to be too many private smiles now. I couldn't be sure so I stopped smiling just in case and went to sleep in relative peace, everything having pretty much balanced out to facilitate a feeling of neutrality like nothing good or bad had ever happened.

The next morning we woke to an eeriness that clung to the boat, as a thick mist clung to the boat, and we could just make out some shadowy cliffs and strange noises that echoed through the air. With such freshness and eeriness at hand, we all decided we must take advantage of the ambiance and have a walk about out on deck after breakfast and at several other intervals throughout the morning. The mathematician kept pretending he didn't want to join us out on deck. But we knew it was because he'd elected not to bring any spare warm clothing or other extras.

"Were you trying to impress people by packing really light?" D asked as we marched back inside cheerily, for the third or fourth time.

"Really not." he replied from his lonely interior seating position.

But the level of conviction in his tone was simply too low.

"So why did you pack so unnecessarily light then," D pressed on, "and look really smug about it on the descent to the boat as multiple comrades around you were struggling with heavy loads?"

"Yeah you shouldn't try to brag about packing light," I added, "for some, packing light requires psychological training et cetera that they just haven't yet had the time to accomplish."

I found myself eyeing up Djako as I finished; so far he seemed to have brought exactly the right amount of stuff and it was annoying; how did this clown achieve things… that even a mathematician could not? We weren't alone though; the night before, it had come to light that the inspector had forgotten to pack any spare trousers as he'd arrived at the fancy dinner in his shorts, sporting a ruthless and jittery attitude that felt particularly savage. We'd chosen not to bring up the shorts situation in front of him therefore, but rather just enjoyed thinking about it with satisfaction instead, as it's nice to have little recurring confirmations that others are struggling too.

As the boat pushed on through the mist that morning, the sound of bells came drifting through from up ahead somewhere, and sure enough the flicker of light and shadow of civilisation came creeping into view as we pushed on through the grey towards it.

"Land HOOO!" Djako called.

"You're no pirate or sea general." the inspector growled, "Hold your tongue boy."

I thought this was a good response, and Djako looked disappointed, which confirmed the validity of the thought. We all came out on deck again to watch the town approach, and even the mathematician ventured out this time; one of the dancers had taken pity and leant him a shawl of some kind. The faint call of harbourmen could be heard along with the clinking of sail poles and other sea-related stuff.

"Resupply stop!" announced the captain, "We'll be sheltering here a while."

And we crept into the harbour to disembark and explore the town.

9

WE ROAMED A WHILE this town, where lay quaint avenues lined by chocolatiers and curious boutiques, until we stumbled on a little shop of ancient things with no use no more except for that of memory, yearning, desire and awe. It was a crooked place, nestled between two cobbled streets, just as a shop of this sort should be. So we shuffled straight on in, barely conscious of the choice, but only doing as is fit when wandering fine old towns that safeguard nooks and crannies, narrow streets, and well-worn ground.

"Hey look!" the banker cried, "That's surely that clearing where we lunched out on the grass, there on this old map…"

We bustled over to take a look and verify this hefty claim before glancing at each other in satisfied surprise amidst murmured agreement.

"Yeah, there's the tracks along the lake…"

"And the little station marked in the clearing there!"

Until cold water was poured *ad libitum* — or so the banker chose precise — upon our cheerful musings.

"That's an old fool's map," the shopkeeper chuckled, "a treasure map, a thing of fantasy and dreams!"

"But we've gone through there we're sure of it — we took a train!" the banker cried again, "This ad libitum chuckling of yours is purely speculative! We saw two strangers pass — they no doubt found it too!"

"Oh men have gone searching for it but none have returned," the shopkeeper continued, "all lost to time and space — all lost men — there's no cosy stations or train tracks to guide the way round these parts."

"That could explain why they were weird," D murmured, "maybe they're just lost men, perpetually reviewing restaurants."

"Mmmm," Djako nodded in solemn agreement, "adibitum ghosts and dead men."

"Well we're alive enough, surely?" the banker affirmed with strained conviction before turning more sternly to Djako, "And don't misuse the *ad libitum* please."

"Yeah and we don't believe in ghosts anyway do we?" I asked to clarify, while working out whether Djako had done some kind of linguistic joke or was just worse than thought, "...or this perpetual stuff?"

"Come on now," the shopkeeper chuckled on at us, "you travellers need a drink — out you go now, I'm closing up."

"How much for the map?"

"More than you can imagine." he snapped, banging his countertop shut again and ushering us to the door, "Out! Cease searching quandary where all would otherwise be sound — be gone and be this sound under the magic of the night!"

"Anyway," I turned to ask the banker as I thought about his Latin stuff and still processed the shopkeeper's words, "how do you know about Latin stuff?"

"Train guard gave me some private lessons after I expressed interest in use cases following his pre-Great Ascent speech."

"Oh OK." I said, and wasn't sure whether to feel impressed or just weirded out as I observed him a moment or two before sensing the pressing glare of the shopkeeper.

So having gazed out the window a bit to verify the magic whilst resignedly concluding Djako's *ad libitum* misuse was likely far off any kind of joke due to lack of acknowledgement through collective giggling or even just meek grinning from the banker who looked learned, we followed the sound advice and ventured out into the night, faring on without looking back to the sound — a proper one this time — of *tring*, as the little shop door swung shut.

"But don't shop doors only go *tring* when you open them?" the banker remarked as we turned the corner to leave.

"Ermmm... yeah." I said while having a think, "That sounds right."

So we stopped and peered back round the corner, in a subtle manner so we wouldn't be seen to be snooping. And there were silhouettes in the shop, grouped around the map we'd been admiring.

"That's annoying," D muttered as we turned again to resume our leaving of this place, "he said he was closing up…"

I woke the next morning in an old auberge we'd taken a liking to the night before, and having ventured down to find the morning room, I found myself breakfasting alone, still reflecting on the map, but also in conversation with the proprietor whom I was dejectedly deciding liked to campaign against ideas of breakfasting in peace.

"You've been here before," he said, "aye, years I'd say you walked these streets."

I looked up and thought, *maybe this campaigner's right… I mean he can't be because I've not been here before… but maybe it's possible this clown is right*, because a funny sensation came upon me as his words rang through the air.

And so this became the day I'd leave this place I'd dwelled so long, allegedly, and yet that I would only come to know then for the first time. For I took to town that day, to wander now from street to street with no direction due, and feel the walls, and cobbled floors, and all the little quaint decors like they knew that I was there this time and we'd become a strangely one. And each step came ever lightly like a scampering on a cloud must be with feeling dancing freely to and fro, just as spring rabbits play and patter mountain meadows, suffering no bad or good or some other made-up would or could; there was only one dance here with no movement right or wrong.

And after the streets and I were done with one another, next came the park that rose and calmly stood atop this bustling town, where it looked across the spires and muddled rooftops, and then the other way, to the lonely peaceful mountain sitting hazy on the plain. And there in that spot, silent tears came and rallied in surprise a warm relief — only a small trickle that ran down lightly unopposed as I stood bewildered and disarmed. No tear of grief or gladness, but rather those of appreciation for the greatness and deep privilege of being permitted to feel; realisation, for what seemed the first time, of this great wave of feeling that rolls around with such sheer force; how one might be brought to tears and laughter in unison for no other reason than encountering an improbable peace, when for a fleeting moment, weary emotions scattered once so far by the meddlesome mind, find common ground upon which to join again in unison, as they were surely always meant to be. Because I was softly laughing now through the gentle tears, at this observation of mind's folly perhaps, but too just at this ease of being when one felt without divide. So I walked on a while whilst holding tight this un-divide, finding the detail of the feeling hardly mattered; the detail was not but words like *good* or *sad*, and small ideas of fad we like to entertain; small ripples on a wave which possessed never need of dissection; a whole heaving giant that undulates and swells, but always is as one and only tamed when one and unassailed by conceited, calculating minds that wish to divide, to categorise, and conquer in cold blood.

And even now the wave is sweeping by as I look on; in strangely comforting and incontestable fashion it's passing by so nonchalant. Well I could never have tamed it anyway; it's rolling on until it will be gone one day, when it fulfilled its destiny of mortality which did make it worthwhile, or when it was just no longer willed to be.

I came to sense company had joined me then, and turned to find the banker, Djako, and D at my side, caught up to me at last, and looking out across the plain, engaging in some observing and reflecting, because the view demanded nothing less.

"I wonder if we can get away with celebrating all the sadness and frustration et cetera, or you know, all the bad stuff," I said, wiping my eyes as we drew the view, and glancing irritably at some people who had come up right beside us to look at the view even though there was loads of space further down the wall, "...by simply claiming it's a privilege to feel — the very basis of being alive — the magnitude of the feeling a reminder of the richness of life, whilst the detail of the feeling hardly relevant in the scheme of things?"

"Haha, what are you talking about!?" Djako laughed, giving me a clap on the back, "Come on, lets walk downtown and get into the action, apparently there's a big event on this afternoon!"

I looked round for a word from D in hope of a more reassuring response, but he'd already wandered off to my disappointment. So sighing and half-smiling in voluntary surrender because one can only do so, we turned from our drawing of the view, and headed for the cobbled street that would facilitate an ambling down to town, bring some distress to ankle, and permit some mental satisfaction because it was old and steeped in character and would no doubt bring us there with a fleeting piece of past.

As Djako had promised, the big event materialised once we'd ambled long enough and strayed upon a fair parade that sauntered through the town, which for better or for worse imposed new life on the once-peaceful cobbled streets. But *for better* was confirmed as fair fast grew to great when came the sound of it advancing somewhere close behind the passing columns. With no compromise it came and with no question of authority, while fear was cast to memory where it cowered in a corner. The band it was that came, and non-negotiably at that, for how it played with such a faithfulness, a certainty and style, and how the world knew then that hope had still its army on the way. There were shining clarinets and chords, arrays of trumpeting and horns, all backed by the booming and rattling of drums all shapes and forms, and nothing could stop them now while with such clarity and ease joy ruled across the world as this band marched forth to afflict all present things whether they were wanting it or not. For the beat surged so freely and outrageously unchecked through all it came encounter, be it the mounted ranks in military dress; fair maidens prancing by as blurs of ribboned flowing hair; once-unruly children, who while still ran and rampaged, did so only with the beat now; or not least us simple bystanders plain helpless to resist.

"Dare I say I think the horses feel it too!" the banker cried, "Look at how they dance!"

And just when all seemed as triumphant as could be, the band would be rejoined by the ever so sure bang of the snare which only lifted things still further into insobriety and elation.

"Who else is feeling hopeful?" Djako called out above the fray.

And we cheered quite raucously, against our better judgement, because we weren't the type to front a brouhaha in any standard situation, but it felt kind of good, and simply fitting for the moment.

"What are they doing over there?" D shouted, because we were shouting, as a loud bang went off, "…It looks like they're blowing stuff up!"

"Yeah it looked like a snowman or something!" I roared back without restraint.

And we took a little time to wonder, whether like our brouhahaing, this was apt as well — the blowing up of stuff — because neither this would seem that sound in any standard situation, though gentle brouhahaing hardly contended as a misdemeanour next to offhand pyrotechnics.

As we pushed through the throng to investigate further, to our delight we discovered some delicious-looking food stalls upon reaching the blow-up area. But our money wasn't accepted so we couldn't get anything, and the blowing up of stuff had stopped. So a bit disheartened and insobriety wearing off, we retreated back through the streets towards the boat and reflected on how we forgot that time and money were big ruling-of-world participants too, alongside that of joy, hope and other made-up stuff.

"Must have been the excitement of the live music…" D muttered as we tried to justify the potentially unwarranted elation.

"Yeah," the banker added wistfully, "and those prancing maidens with the ribbons…"

Anyway, happening upon a rustic-looking tavern as we wound back through the streets, we decided to therapise through tomato and vodka-based cocktails accompanied by a bowl of high-quality olives that acted as an apero.

"Can we get some tomato and vodka-based cocktails please?" Djako asked the barman gaily.

"Do you mean Bloody Marys?" he grunted back looking slightly fed up.

"Yes, those!"

So happily taking up comfortable seating positions, we got cosy and thought about some stuff to say to pass away the time. In addition, as a bonus bit of intrigue not long later, we found ourselves observing someone waiting to be served and agreed it was amusing since he'd been waiting for *aaages*!

"Sorry for the wait." the barman finally said to him.

"That's OK," he replied with ease, "I was just standing here, enjoying myself."

We looked on a while, in astonishment, reeling from this seemingly super-human response/claim.

"...Maybe he's decoupled and disidentified from his mind," the banker suggested, "and is become truly conscious, revelling now in awareness and the unsullied essence of life."

"What," D responded nonchalantly, yet with an air of intrigue, "umm... how do you get about achieving that?"

We all leant in to listen.

"Not sure." the banker replied, as he looked on wistfully to the horizon.

"Hmmm..." we hummed back in unison as we took a

moment to consider.

"Maybe they're just mad." I ventured.

After some further looking on a while, we agreed that we'd hope they were just mad in order so we'd have less to want for, and so that we might reserve jealousy for other, more trivial things which were more comforting to be jealous of. Like who's got the best hair/legs, or who knew more about fire-lighting techniques and historical battles like Austerlitz or Rorke's Drift.

Then in quiet reflection, gently harassed by feelings of uncertainty, we took refuge in our books and read while Djako seemed to think recounting American-Indian historical battles was appropriate. But we were reading and those ones lacked strategy, or he just didn't know it. Due to his determination though, he continued to recount with greater success when we went on to dine because book refuge was inaccessible, and it turned out the banker knew a bit about the strategy, although it was clearly lacking in general compared to proper Napoleonic ones or ones that the British were in.

"Yeah, so little strategy involved in these battles though." D lazily interjected, "Not like Austerlitz where there was loads."

"Yeah, or Rorke's Drift!" I added with a bang, or what felt like could have been one, as I looked around triumphantly, though traction this bang gained was less than I'd have liked because it didn't gain any.

As dining and debating wound down, thoughts of a cosy night crept along as we conversed quietly to one another in the post-dinner lounge. But to our dismay, we heard a noise come to addle the quiet clink of coffee cup and soft rustling of pages turn — only faint at first — almost a sure figment of the imagination it was. But yes, it was the calling of the band, the brass band that paraded; it was someway off, but it was sure! Without further ado, we laid down our miserable old books, threw defeatist pre-bed coffee cups back to the tabletops whence they came, and took to the streets of this strange town to fall quarry to the night. We picked our way down cobbled lamp-lit streets, softly slipping through the cold night air, and sure enough, after some twisting and turning, and double backing here and there, we fell upon the shining marching ranks. In as much formation as ever, harassing at free will the city's heart, they were pushing on and playing still triumphantly, undefeated without fear; the relentlessness was blinding, and the strategy no doubt profound we could agree, as they paraded on the moonlit streets to thwart the would-be nothingness. And the world seemed march with them, with little qualm or care.

After a while of nighttime parading which we all got pretty good at, we decided we'd heard all the songs, so we found a bar in this relentless town of chocolatiers and perpetual parades and ordered some drinks. It was too expensive and also turned out to be the same bar as before and we got reminded about how we were just constantly getting conned all the time no matter how we set about.

"You know," D said looking down at his legs, "did I really need a new pair of trousers? It's what the world keeps on saying, but I'm not so sure."

We all had a look at his legs/trousers and nodded in thought.

"Yeah, I bought a clip to put money in not so long ago," Djako added, "I was led to believe it would make me look good and that it was also practical."

"Never used it?" I leisurely confirmed.

"Nahhh..." he sighed back, "don't even know where it is."

"And they're always making up more money." the banker added.

"Ohhh, surely more money's a good thing?" Djako replied.

"Nahhh, it's just another con."

"Yeah and the education system too." D said.

"Is it?" a guy waiting at the bar called over as we looked up to see it was the same one waiting as before.

"Yeah they're just teaching us stuff that's not even useful and distracting us from stuff that matters."

"What about voting and democracy and fair society type stuff?" he called back over.

"What do you think?" the barman said, deciding to join in.

"Is that rhetorical?" D called back.

"What do you think?" the barman said again, raising his eyebrows like he'd been all here before.

"Yeah, it's rhetorical — suggesting belief in swindle." the guy waiting at the bar nodded solemnly, "I know that tone... but con or not, I don't mind — I'm just standing here enjoying myself."

So then we took a few sips of our tomato-based cocktails

in silence as we wondered about all the ways we'd been getting conned these passing years and how we'd continue to be getting so, and how this guy who stands around just enjoying himself probably was definitely mad; there was no other way.

"So let me tell you a story," the banker commenced as the cocktails took effect/conned us and so cleared the way for us to get cosy near the fire and forget about troubling things/things that mattered.

While we prepared to answer, he continued to commence.

"I was a boy once…"

"Hmmm." D sceptically outed, but it didn't put the banker off.

"…Mmm, yes. And I knew a girl whom I loved, but she didn't love me back. So do you know what I did? I took her on a train — not our train, another one I think — and came to a place just like this, just like this strange town… yes, that's right, I think I've been here before!"

A short pause ensued, offering us the chance perhaps to gasp or proceed with some other acknowledgement of surprise. Just as we decided to do the acknowledgment though, a swively armchair beside us, tall enough to conceal its sitter who had no doubt been gazing broodily into the depths of the flickering fire before them, swivelled round to reveal the inspector, his features dazzling us as they were highlighted by the dancing light of flame. And this combination rendered his entrance to the conversation really dramatic and surprising.

"...So have you been here before then," he grunted without enthusiasm, "or do you just *think* you have?"

The banker decided to ignore the question, and continued determinedly on, leaving the scowling inspector, and his slightly obsoleted dramatic entrance, in his wake.

"...Yes, this looks strangely familiar — I took her to this very bar I'd have thought, where the drinks were too expensive. And she adored it! She was so impressed that she decided to reciprocate her love for me that very day. Mind you, I did demand her assurance that it was me and not just the expenditure of money she loved. And she did indeed confirm with rapidity. So... there we are my friends, surprised?"

"Well hold on," I queried, "what happened to the girl?"

"She's my wife of course!" he said and looked at us smiling triumphantly.

"HA!" D laughed, "That's the worst story of romance I've ever heard! BORING and she clearly just loves the money and the holidaying!"

"You SON OF A BITCH!" the banker roared.

And with face purpling, and body rearing, he knocked D out cold on the floor, the live action partially making up for the low-quality story. Djako and I looked at the body, probably deciding what to do, and so did the inspector with a drunk looking nod and grunt.

"...So have you been here before or not?" Djako ventured in order to wrap things up.

"I don't give a damn!" the banker retorted, and sitting down, took a swig of whisky before falling into silent reflection.

So with a dormant D laid beside us, and a story-time-concluding *cheers!* slurred from the re-swivelled armchair, we decided to do the same for a while in a surprisingly peaceful silence, only broken by the soothing crackle of fire and an occasional hiccup.

"So who's actually swindling us then?" Djako asked to break the quiet.

"What do you mean?" D croakily replied having slipped warily back into his chair by now.

"I mean we were just saying we're always getting conned all the time whatever we try and do," he continued, "but who's actually behind it all, where are they? Because then we can take them down."

"Oh why's your solution always taking people down?" the banker snapped.

"There's no one specific conning us," slurred the inspector's voice from out behind his armchair, "the system is faceless — it's the result of billions of humans slash things carrying out trillions of interactions in real time and over millions of years powering the evolution of the unstoppable system as we know it. So you're fighting no one but millions of things and years and nature itself."

"What…" D said, "how do you know so much about systems?"

"That artist woman told me." he grunted back.

"Oh, I was thinking it sounded a bit more mathematiciany."

"Nahhh, he doesn't comment on stuff like that — he's not enough sure his words."

"Hmmm," Djako murmured, "I reckon if we take down

some key players we can bring it all down and sail into the sunset."

"What time were we meant to get back to the boat?" I asked abruptly as I'd been brooding about whether I'd been here before because how come the banker had maybe been here too? And that auberge guy seemed pretty convincing. And what if it was just a con…

"Oh yeah, it's getting pretty late," D said, eyes flicking up in thought, "I sort of assumed they'd come get us."

"Who's they?" the inspector grunted from his chair.

"The authorities or whoever."

"There's no authorities in this town," he slurred back, "bands rampaging through the street, blowing stuff up, it's a disgrace!"

"Maybe we should wander back to the port," I suggested, "and see what's going on."

So we wandered back together, marvelling or grumbling about things, depending on the person and the moment. It turned out they'd been waiting for us for *aaages* and everyone seemed pretty annoyed.

"What have you idiots been doing!?" one of the dancers was shouting, "We've been waiting for aaages!"

"There was no instructions!" the inspector barked back, "It's chaos here!"

So we boarded back on amongst grumblings and scolding stares, and the boat slipped away with us into the dark of the fjord.

"Yeah," we muttered, "appalling organisation."

"Who goes out drinking late at night when they know

there's surely a boat waiting for them?" the dancers continued.

"I dunno..." D mumbled disappointedly.

"Yeah somehow things got all magical and merry..." I added, but to no real sympathy.

"Yerrr could of just stood there waiting, enjoying yerselvvves," Djako suggested hopefully but with an unseemly slurring, "yer know, decoupling from errrrrr... revelling now and unsullied things... wwhha—"

"What the hell are you talking about you oaf!" the dancer snapped back at him, "Get back to your cabin now!"

So we slunk back to our cabins and bed, wishing for better allies/arguments.

The next morning we woke to calls on deck and ventured out to see what all the fuss might be about.

"Take these sails down!" the captain was bellowing, "Burn them! We cannot want for wind when we know no direction by which to want for!"

"Yeah!" Djako screamed, "Take 'em down till it's time to march on, when the sun goes down behind the trees and the sky is red with the tears of old dreams and high hopes that bleed so freely."

"WHAT THE FECK IS GOING ON?!" the inspector screamed back wild eyed, and sounding Irish — maybe he was actually.

"I don't know what this chap is saying," the captain replied, "but we're taking down these sails, and we're burning them. We go with the current now."

And the sails started burning, and we all watched them burn as we stood on deck, silently, and surprisingly calmly.

"What was that shit?" D asked Djako as we watched, "Why were you getting involved in boat management matters?"

He looked pensively back, surprised at himself — embarrassed even — with a shuffling of foot.

"Not sure…"

"Were you… trying to deliver another one of your over-optimistic speeches?" I murmured to him.

But, I think he pretended not to hear me.

The boat went on a while longer and the fjord we were following steadily grew narrower and narrower until it didn't look like the boat would even fit anymore.

"It doesn't look like the boat's even going to fit anymore." someone called, as we stood on the front deck gazing at the steadily encroaching rock walls.

But the captain wasn't interested or didn't hear, and a few moments later we'd ground to a halt, the boat stuck against the rock on either side.

"Everybody off!" the captain called.

"What," an alarmed mathematician queried, "is this normal?"

"Perfectly normal," the captain replied, "just a standard docking and disembarking manoeuvre, everybody off!"

So we hastened off in some degree of disarray, but it seemed to work as there was a sort of passage cut into the cliff which we found ourselves following, leading out of the fjord and to a cobbled lane which took us on, to leave the boat, the sea, and the strange old town behind us.

"I wonder how he gets the boat back out again..." I deliberated out loud as we walked away.

"Probably just goes into reverse." D replied.

It was a ghostly place, this, where the paved lane ran. Where lampposts glowed through still fog that seemed dare not move or swirl for the shapes and shadows beneath it might expose to those from the land of the living who passed through, and who weren't ready to believe. And footsteps sounded louder on the cobbled street than they would a usual one, and echoed not, but disappeared to die alone out there, beyond the narrowness that we were bound to here. Down to the little station the cobbled street led, through no man's land and surely as our only friend at hand. A crow would call from here and there, and flutter softly by, overhead or to one side — shadows and shapes to our eyes at times when those dared flutter too close to unknown's edge. And a fragrant smell of smoke and fallen leaves, mushrooms, and other damp things hung about the air; it had to be autumn in this ghostly place.

The station was no less ghostly, for it too was lonely and neglected. Where an old sign gently swayed and creaked, crows came to land and caw, and look down on us, in pity, or just with no empathy at all; we could be prey to some werewolf from folklore, or just the passengers on a train; for them it hardly mattered either way. And knowing this, it made the place haunting, yet so real and relatable — a place that sang in unison with the rawness and mercilessness of bare desire, for it told what felt like truth.

"This is surely a ghost train that we await this time." Djako uttered with unease as he looked around hesitantly.

"Well it's supposed to be the same train as before." I pointed out.

"Maybe the people running it have been rogue ghosts all along." the inspector growled, "Their disregard for rule and documentation suggests no less."

We couldn't be certain if he was joking or not as we were all feeling uneasy and susceptible to tall tales and fantasy.

"Maybe it only picks up ghosts." D said.

"...But that would mean that we're ghosts." Djako said with wider eyes than normal.

"Haha," D laughed, "well then it wouldn't matter cos we don't even know it."

We all had a bit of a shiver then, due to the cold in part only. And so we rubbed our hands together, blew into them a bit, and stamped feet here and there. This boosted morale/confidence levels and made us all feel a bit more jolly and cosy. It also proved an effective medium to long-term waiting technique as it took us safely through to the sound of a distant train approaching, hooting somewhere in the depths of the forest beyond, out from which it would steam.

So we waited expectantly on the platform and did a bit of chatter, the quality of which never really got that high; waiting at train stations was never a moment destined for high-quality conversation. Perhaps it's the waiting for something — the pressing expectation in one's mind for the next stage to begin — which means the in-between stage that the platform is doomed to be, is never quite come to peace with. At last the train arrived, exactly on time supposedly, and with a wave of relief, we got on, as the in between was surely no more, for the moment.

It was more relaxing now as we understood the train; we all had our respective seating positions and tables and areas which had become synonymous with each of us. So no childish boarding rush and mad seat acquisition was necessary — something that we'd agreed, during the previous chatter of the in between, that we'd never engage in anyway.

"Ahhh," the inspector sighed as he came to sit down, "so the waiting rebegins…"

"What do you mean?" D questioned, "I thought we'd just finished the waiting?"

"The waiting for this train to get us there." he retorted in an evident manner.

"Hmm, I'd not been thinking of it like that…"

So maybe we were still in the in between and were doomed to low-quality chatter indefinitely so…. This was a disconcerting thought though, we all agreed, and so we decided to agree that we couldn't possibly still be in the in between; it would be far too degenerate to fall for such state of mind.

10

THROUGH GREAT BROKEN lands our slender way wound forward, upon which the train held fast but only just, as sharp slopes and crumbled castles came impose upon and coax our view; on a hill sometimes, far off, but up close too, where gnarled trees grew and rabbits burrowed in the broken roots of these old safe places. And faded bracken lay exhausted, cracking into dust, with only faint memory of green barely hanging through these darker months. It was all broken this land and scarred by fallen shattered rock exposed now to the mercy of the open air and standing sure no more.

Oh how it's all broken now, we thought, *unfixably broken*; even by hands that know how to fix, hands that heal and hark hope. But these hands are no good to us now, no gods, no sun or rain, or even early morning birdsong however joyful and triumphant. No woodsmoke that drifts through morning mist to spark senses and call us to the café and the hot tea that's steaming and the cakes and the scones and the toast that's battered and all the while the logs are burning and crackling softly in the hearth. But no soft crackle can save us now, surely, no flicker of flame, or creaking of a coach that's trundled over marsh and moor as darkness was descending, to find shelter for tired travellers in a worn-out inn that's held alone so long a barren hillside yet roars defiant welcome still, and seems to smoulder memory born from old embers of cold lonely nights and howling winds, to treasured tales of distant wanderers that came and went before.

So what on earth will save us now? rampaged the question through the carriages. A fairytale kiss from gallant knight or paling princess, or just someone we loved once and maybe did yet still again? A kind word that all is well, however void the flailing word may be? A mother and a father, reunited and smiling once more, just like they always used to? Or perhaps the sun, or the sound of rain pitter-pattering on leaves, or on a tent, or on some other roof over our heads and below the stars that were shining all along.

I was broken today, and I didn't know why; we all were, and we knew not why. The train was creaking, the sky looked cracked, why the food seemed all rotten and the drink gone sour. Conversation proved trivial as there was nothing to be said that had not already been said somewhere or in some way. Even the violinist couldn't play, or rather the notes were all wrong; his hands trembled so, unfit for his once-majestic bow. The birds didn't fly; were they just walking today or what? And the sun shined but it wasn't hot or cold; the temperature intangible and the light unrequired as it shone onto nothing of use. What was this place of nothingness — it didn't even look less full to the eye, than a place of fullness, so how had this nothingness come to be?

Nevertheless, all defeated and exposed, we went forward, to do our duty as something that exists; all broken by unknowns and miscomprehensions, and lost quests for illumination, we went forward because such seems be the nature of to be which presumably is reason enough to advance; whilst we knew such days were only standard and might well come on suddenly as we reflected on that devious hotel where passed just another noticeably lesser day than could have been. And also the choice was somewhat limited, so the reason we made up hardly mattered.

"Yeah as long as the train keeps advancing, we'll be OK." the banker said as we peered out at the broken land that seemed to slow our speed.

"Why?" D asked, "What will happen if it stops advancing?"

"Well..." he spluttered back, "then we'd be stuck here in no man's land!"

"But what would actually change whether we're on the train here or on the train there?"

"Well, we wouldn't be advancing! We'd be festering!"

And I wondered whether there really was a difference between the advancing and the festering as I looked to D to question again, although he was taking too long.

"What's the difference between the advancing and the festering then?" I asked.

"Mathematician?" Djako suggested.

"Nah, his numbers are no use here." D said, "Look how

he's lost in thought over there — he's more broken than us."

"The difference is we have no choice but to advance," the inspector growled as he nodded out the window, "otherwise we'd be doing nothing, stuck in a state of inaction and slowly crumbling to join this blasted broken land."

"We're gonna slowly crumble either way." D replied.

"No, look, we're pushing on to finer pastures!" Djako exclaimed, "Even the bison know that — the moose, and the deer — they're all pushing on across the plains, to finer pastures each new year!"

"Yeah," the mathematician mumbled as he too stared on and out the window lost in thought, "there is no other way."

Though with gazes transfixed by the land without, we had to wonder why we couldn't stop but look and feel a twang in heart; discern how things grew in harmony through the rock and ruins, making that which stood before indeed more magic. In fact, this place was full of joy and in no need of fixing, proving more savvy than a priest and a mathematician and a banker combined, not to mention the rest of us; for our concord could not hope compete with its. So this broken land we hastened through seemed not that broken after all; maybe all the brokenness only lay within the limits of the train. But it was a recognition too beautiful, and too disturbing, for our calculations to bear. Yes, we had to push on, advance on and past this place, before it proved us moot; before it quenched our thirst for more and stayed us on a fine rock where we'd fret forever after in a safe and peaceful place.

So in the end yes, we pushed on through this broken land, then more places, through the highs and lows, and all the bits laid in between. And it was all endured with content or without, with heroics or without, and with courage or without; it made no difference either way. It was endured because there was no other way. And for this final reason, we could continue simply and peacefully, for no other reason was needed, as none other, however seductive, could be true.

"Can someone help us with these cases?" one of the dancers called out as we were wandering up and down corridors one morning, engaging in simple and peaceful continuation to the best of our ability due to lack of other way.

The guard popped his head round their compartment door and peered in.

"I could offer you that muscle come made of fine words and dulcet tones," he kind of sang, "like a songbird — *nay* — a lark — who hovers on high a mountain breeze, spectating so, that of brute force and heavy hand which festers down below."

"Wha—" they started in response.

"Et oui," the guard quickly cut them off, "vos valises seraient toutes déplacées, ne serait-ce que dans un monde qui a — là — 'fin — jadis, ou sinon quasiment tout juste, transcendé tous les apparats du domaine physique épuisé — mais ce serait beau tu vois quand même."

And then he just strolled off chuckling down the corridor, giving us a nod on his way. We looked at the dancers standing silent in their compartment door and felt a bit sorry for them.

"Did he just speak Fr—"

"YOU LOOK EVER SO FORLORN!" Djako shouted at them while cutting me off, "Why the sorry faces?"

"I think it's because they're confused by the train guard's behaviour." I pointed out while considering, or possibly un-wilfully admiring, his widening apparent linguistic ability, although I guessed he would have been well-travelled, although that still couldn't really account for the Latin, unless he was really old... and then I thought about those perpet-ual dead men, and the ghostly station not long past, and that fucking aubergist who said disturbing and uncanny things and wouldn't just let me eat the cornflakes in peace so I'd have been able to effectively decide between tea and coffee, because I ended up choosing coffee, but I think I wanted tea — I nearly always get tea in the morning. And then I hotly continued, "...He doesn't appear to have helped them does he, he's just confused them."

"Is it because of the train guard's behaviour?" Djako bluntly asked as they looked at him not nicely, "Is it because he's appeared not to have helped you? Because if you knew a little dialect and were feeling kind of playful, in another world you'd just be quasi-thankful — *nay* — a-quasi-smitten by his dreaming and grand commentary."

What the hell, I thought while watching him apparently joining in the fun, as adding to the already developing dis-concertion, I suddenly got a nasty feeling he actually understood what the train guard had said, and maybe had a knowledge I did not, a sophistication I'd have liked, and also maybe that this meant he actually was half-French, even though I didn't think his knowledge on Napoleonic warfare strategy supported this. And this still didn't account for the other two halves. So I got a bit stuck in thought and phased out slightly because things had become too difficult to process. Anyway, our sight can't have been high quality because the dancers continued looking at us in a manner that wasn't nice along with a hint of bewilderment, so we decided to help them with their cases while discussing how, on balance, it had been a relatively exciting event and probably would be the most exciting event for a while.

As days and nights passed, further great cocktails of sensation came to consume our advancing carriages; some ingenious that could have been given a lasting name, and some just ill-conceived; either way they let us know we were alive. Like great merriment, mild serenity, tired confusion, additional train guard encounters, or just plain bad ones like when staying up to talk, laugh, drink away looming niggles of mind, and continue the endurance of consciousness, seemed fruitless. Ones where it seemed the only refuge was bed and a lonesome sleep where travel through dreams and nightmares would be possible, with no regret or grief, or familiar feeling of inexplicable guilt, as you could know, after, that they were only dreams and nightmares. This well-earned right to bask in the immunity they provide was gladly invoked numerous nights of several, to attain their last safe haven. Like an abandoned hut on a mountainside, only enduring so it might save a weary walker as the night was coming down; or maybe just like an impenetrable den built when things were simpler, because even though it wasn't impenetrable, you could still believe it was.

"You're going to bed early." someone noted on one of those fretful nights.

"I know I am." I mumbled back.

"How come?"

I mumbled some more stuff in return, perhaps already feeling some unwarranted guilt as mind continued to slip further into depths of fragility, and positive expectant faces were inescapably present. Only able to wonder at how I'd slipped from high places, or where Djako, D, and others seemed be, I stumbled down the rolling corridor that didn't deign to pity, but that would facilitate an arrival to somewhere peaceful. To where all would be guarded and sunken, and retreated under covers that ask no questions; to where bed will be come, unconsciousness will be, and a strange persistence we might call guilt, or some other regrettable sensation, can hang above it, or below, but either way be safely abandoned for a while beyond this refuge where thought will be beset no more.

So in position primed for sleep/highland refuge and with anticipation teeming, a fantastic succession of dreams/nightmares would come to shake the little sleeping compartment that night, interspersed by vague consciousness adorned by the comfort of the rock and clank of train and the little noises that those objects without the luxury of stabilisation are obliged to emit through it all even when the rest of us are silent and sleeping and dreaming in the dark that demands it.

...Yes! Up to that rock there! Look how it sits so sturdy, and there how long it must have sat. We'll bound up there for it's calling us, though the slope below it may be slippy and tricky and fraught with sticks and stones unshown that could break bone or brave ankle on its way. So we'll take an ounce of care along the way, yes, though not too much less it dampen bounce to naught but a steady picking of way which wouldn't feel the same; could never be the same.

"Hey there!" someone will surely call amidst a breath or two for pause, "...Wait for me!"

Haha, and one would only glance back with a chuckle and wave over shoulder before pushing on — bounding up and on to where glory surely be.

The sun is shining now the rock is reached; its final rays are falling over us and lighting up our rock like the heart of this wild land. And the last of us are scrambling up the final steps of this damn slope that nearly had us all but could never really have had us at all as we were those of high spirits and hope. *Good man! Good man!* and other words of friendship are called and clapped upon as the last of us arrives and takes a seat atop this rock forever strong and steady on the ever-shifting slope.

So now we'll sit and watch the sun go down as it marks for us, this place, in shadow and in light; watching beauty softly pale away before the rallying of the night as the light passed by behind the stars somewhere. And under the moon by now, we'll sit and have a drink as the rock has still not wavered, and we'll listen to things of the dark like hoots and ticks of nightly things and gentle trickles of worn-out streams that don't know sleep for the world did never will it. And when we lie down because we got tired or just felt an ache somewhere in body or in mind, one will surely tell us tales of the stars and all the signs. And we'll find it like a fairy tale, or something nigh on magic, and wonder why we never thought to learn of starry magic things ourselves; maybe it wasn't really that interesting when we were in another place, in our world of mind that came to err.

Oh and some of us are brave now, for we are drunk, and so we move on from this rock which has been holding us so well, to higher places that we don't know so well and can't see now in the dark that's come. We'll keep climbing though, until we can climb no more, or until we decide we just don't need to anymore, for who's waiting up there anyway…

I woke the next day thinking about rocks and slopes and nightly things; if only I'd gotten further up that hillside I could have found out more stuff, I was sure. I looked at Djako and privately blamed him for scuppering such fantasies with his abominable attempts at implementing quiet wake-up routines and extracting himself from this damn cabin of a room that was surely stifling me and all from greater things; high horizons that were destined me.

…Oh, up to that rock that will ask us no question or demand, nor inane impossibility; it will only beckon us and then hold us up high, but not too high mind, since it's only halfway up or so, keeping soundly safe ourselves from that which reigns above and yonder. And composed and calm we'll surely be as the rock cares not to judge, the rock is…

Go—

Naahh, I thought, *it's not working now I'm awake and conscious of dastardly things like cabinmates and questions and self-centred whims.*

...So to the breakfast hall, to the porridge bowl, to the cold face of the great day that's beckoning; this great mountain of a day that could have been such a small mound of well-turned earth if only one willed it so. So let's will it so; over the porridge bowl, with steaming cup of tea in hand, this breakfast hall will beam...

"Oi," Djako said while poking me, "what are you doing?"

I'd fallen asleep over my porridge bowl and got porridge everywhere. So feeling particularly annoyed, I decided there was no winning sometimes, while the morning ahead seemed like it might be long.

But, with recovery attempts no doubt floundering after what would likely be this long morning, I plotted how I might go on to lunch alone in the glory of peace and non-expectation to appease the lengthy day. Nothing would be asked of oneself, and so no guilt or irritation could be conjured, giving rise to a serenity that would rule a while. Primarily consisting of a cheese sandwich perhaps, yes, cut into triangles, with cheese grated and fatly packing this fluffy conglomerate of crumbs that would be two slices of bread. And there'd be little bits of red onion to make things tingle, and it would be a sandwich of greatness and reconciliation, eaten on one's own terms, how it should be eaten at that moment in time, in a way that could never be relived.

This private and unique cheese-sandwich experience

that ultimately came to fruition managed to lift morale which facilitated the passing of a reasonably relaxed afternoon, before the arms of evening came, and the train rolled to a gentle halt for a period of *compulsory recreational outdoor activity*, as the guard chose exact while he read out from his scroll again and freshly peppered us with perplexing dialect.

Judging by the grey light, the blackness that came from in between the trees, and the way they gently creaked and swayed, I'd say it was a late autumn day, not long before the sun went down. It was nippy, and things rustled and crackled underfoot; things that marked the memory of summer, which while would come again next year, had still been a summer of its own.

We agreed it would be nice to hear an owl hoot from somewhere out there in the cold night air, but the sound never came, until we stopped wanting for it, and then it came, but on half-deaf ears now, for we'd be talking or chuckling or eating then, and letting the world go by in harmony.

"What are you saying it doesn't exist?!" Djako laughed, "Of course it exists!"

"Wull I phink it could be eiver way." the banker said with a mouthful of potato and a wave of his fork.

It was supper time round the campfire, and we were discussing how we might master states of mood, like prolonging bouts of happiness, but also to what end, because what if all the other moods were just as good or maybe even better, seemed to be the newfound question…

"But should we even be striving to be happy?" the mathematician suggested, wildly cutting through the cheery debate, "Will it mean that we led better lives?"

"…Well it would be almost too convenient if it didn't," Djako said, breaking the initial pause for thought, "then we wouldn't have to try and be bloody happy all the time!"

"But you always seem happy…" I said.

"Yeah but it's hard work sometimes." he muttered back, and I had to look at him with less disdain than usual.

"Yeah, is it not only this incessant feeling of duty to be happy that makes us feel incomplete," the banker continued, "because we're not always happy and therefore failing in our duty?"

"Well maybe it is our duty to want to be happy in order to show respect for the life we have been granted?" the mathematician proposed to muddy more the waters, "Even if this seems more likely just another irritating concept we invented to haunt us with consistency…"

"So happiness should just be, or not be, and not amount to much more else." the banker suggested, "Enjoyed and then let go."

Hmmm, yeah, that sounds quite good, I thought, even if I'd heard all this kind of waffle before from a rich array of either greats or clowns, and then forgot it shortly after because it's useless information.

"Yeah so this should let us enjoy happiness while being unreliant on it." I said while trying to get involved in the waffle because there was nothing else to do, and while realising my statement didn't really add much.

"Right, so if we shouldn't be striving for happiness, what should we be striving for?" Djako continued, "Principles? Love? Morality?"

"Morality?" the artist laughed, "You mean a syndrome of guilt and an instinct to survive that's just evolved a little over time? Just look how we gave it credence, a name, endowed it with modernity — made it sound righteous to make ourselves sound earnest — pfffff!"

Yes, she *was* sure of her words. *And hasty*, I thought, *but maybe quite good too*.

"Hmmm," Djako continued, "it's nice to be nice though, which is basically what morality seems to be."

"Though if it turns out it is a great concept we thought of," the mathematician added, "then it's surely infinite, with no end — no ultimate morality."

"Yeah," Djako chuckled, "I suppose man can only ever hope to get halfway up that mountain."

"Halfway up infinity?" D said, "How does that work?"

"Ladder." Djako snapped, looking at him wildly, which actually brought D's mockery to its knees in a strange way.

"Hold on, so morality is either infinite and so impossible to attain," I said after enjoying Djako's snapping, "or nothing, i.e. just a syndrome of guilt and instinct. And so still impossible to attain…"

"Yeah that's pretty bad odds." D said.

"Hmmm, what about love then?" Djako asked.

"Don't even start." an array of voices quickly replied to some relief.

"Soooo…" Djako continued, "will having been happy

mean we led better lives or not?"

"Well we've got to get into the concept of what better is now haven't we." the mathematician started, before getting interrupted as the clamour of ideas pushed on.

"What about if I said that having been sad means we led better lives?" one of the dancers then surprisingly proposed, because usually they sabotaged this kind of stuff, although maybe they were just trying to sabotage through the sowing of confusion, "Would we then all try and be sad, and perhaps feel bad when we were happy?"

"Hmmm," the banker hummed, "that sounds rather negative though."

"Hold on!" Djako cried, "So imagine feeling content when feeling sad, because we've convinced ourselves feeling sad is a good thing? That could solve the problem of feeling sad!"

"Sounds too good to be true." I said, but taking mental note even so, just in case.

"Yeah," D concurred, "there's probably chemical imbalances in the brain that somehow wouldn't allow that, which is a shame."

"Yeahhh…" the artist added, "then again, if you were psychologically strong enough you could neutralise the imbalances with mind power, aka enlightenment."

"Yeah that's it," the inspector darkly muttered, "this happiness-sadness business is irrelevant — it's all about just accepting what is, you know, the enlightenment thing she's saying."

"OK, soooo… will having been happ—"

And the conversation went on, and on, and on, and it got quite tedious in hindsight — yeah, and not in hindsight too — and each had different ideas about various things, and no one really understood or listened to each other particularly well. And it had all been said before countless times, somewhere and some way by someone, although whether this made it mundane or not was unclear. Anyway, it all got out of hand in the end. Therefore we agreed we'd pretty much covered/cracked all this and that we should move on to discuss more comforting concepts like the best way to light a fire. Someone actually claimed that you should light it from the top-down. But this attempted contribution was swiftly dismissed, to the contributor's disappointment, because it was ridiculous. A range of other contributions and concepts relating to fire building and flame conservation were then proceeded with and it was reasonably good fun. Except for those who didn't really ever light fires and so for whom it was probably pretty boring. Plus some people complained and made claims that we'd talked about the topic numerous times before, but these claims sounded childish.

After picnicking and debate had died down, we wandered back to the train to arrive in the nick of time, which proved our wandering less liberal than we'd have liked. But perhaps our liking was not learned, for night and its terrors had then just come to fall, our pale dusk now dead as we kept on. Either way, having taken up standard positions in the bar carriage, we let the train speed us on as a row of little dots in the dark against tall tree and mountainside and through haunting autumn night to come. But the faint clinks of glass and rattles of little things amidst the low nattering of carriage folk made it all cosy and safe within, defying all that dark facade without.

So the train continued on, as it had done before, and nothing much seemed change. But as days and nights passed, there came hushed talk, then rampant rumour, of a telltale expedition, for those souls brave enough and of such physical prowess that those heroes might just triumph. Yes, it would be an expedition for the great; a quest that would leave all others in its wake. The train would make a short stop soon, and there, those worthy would have the chance to prove their might through abandoning the comfort of the train and heading into the wild, before rejoining the train on the other side of a great unknown/plateau, to be showered there, presumably, in praise and admiration for having embarked upon and completed such a trial. Those who weren't brave or physically able enough would simply stay on the train and suffer a cosy continuation of things whilst already fading away into history; glory slipping through their fingers and out of lives that would never have seemed much in their day.

Well over several drinks one evening, and after what we agreed was a good period of careful reflection and consideration, we put our names down; we signed up for this great feat, Djako, D, and I. And this made us feel important and great too, which confirmed it was a good idea. The train had also become heavy with reflection and questioning and tired aged deliberating, we'd decided, so now was the time to break free. So we continued with a series of old whiskies and congratulated ourselves over our decision as we entered into high spirits and the night.

11

AND JUST LIKE THAT, before it seemed we'd hardly had a chance to settle in and know the tracks for what they were, the big day had come upon us. For it had been confirmed that Djako, D, and I would take up the challenge of crossing this great plateau on foot and reconvene with the train way over on the other side; and this was the day we'd begin, making it less small than those more standard ones. So we stepped off our train, tight of heart, but strong of will, even if this will was not as certain as one might have liked, and swung on heavy packs that probably weren't even that heavy. As we took a look back at the train and our comrades that spectated us with a little less sorrow than we'd have liked, it seemed then that a fourth, the banker, had elected to come with us, for he had not the air of spectatorship. While eyeing up his build (short/fat), we signalled with shunning hand and harsh word of mouth that this was no suitable challenge for the likes of him, but he must have wanted to prove himself, so, as he and his kit tumbled determinedly towards us, over the sound of the train's final whistle, our warnings and signs of rejection fell on deaf ears; due to the whistle only in part, or in more understandable completeness, we could not know for sure.

We began by assigning ourselves responsibilities. Being the most adept, I assigned myself map possession, navigation, route/schedule planning, and general command. Although because everyone thought the same, this planning and command would turn out to be shared. Being the strongest (physically), Djako was assigned most of the equipment — a very important job he was told. In need of frequent mental distraction, D was given compass, binoculars, pen and paper, as well as a selection of other tools and miscellanea. The banker had brought his own rucksack without consulting with us upon its contents or the assignment of roles, so with the system compromised for better, for worse, or for just no difference, we let him continue as he saw fit under suspicion that he would prove the weak link amidst our ring of steel.

We watched the train pull away, a little forlorn, and were presumably all wondering why we'd agreed to our non-compulsory challenge. As the tireless mobile home we'd come to know disappeared from view, we turned and looked at the mountains before us. We had to wait a few more minutes for D as he had elected to use his binoculars to watch the train disappearing from view and so the farewell process we'd decided to engage in took longer for him.

The mountain range formed a sort of big plateau, with a

small trail, said the map, scampering through it to reach the other side where the confident-looking train tracks would run again after returning from their defeatist detour around the range. You could see snow starting around halfway up the outer slope of the plateau, and below that, dark ground running down to the valley floor and all the way up to the little station office door.

"What can you see?" we asked D as he observed the scene with his binoculars.

"There's snow starting about halfway up the plateau's outer slope, and blackish ground until then."

There was a brief silence as we considered his observations.

"Right." I said while trying to maintain hope, "Let's go."

And we set off.

The little path that led away from the station was easy enough to follow and we were in high spirits, maybe because there was no one telling us what to do or complaining at us anymore. Djako was singing poorly with Americanesque optimism, D was murmuring contentedly about things, and I was thinking about fire-lighting techniques and how I'd follow an alternative belief system where feeling sad and miserable meant I was succeeding in life so that I could be at peace when such assailants arrived, while I could just forget about this alternative belief system when I was happy because I'd be feeling too good to give a damn. *How invincible I'd be*, I thought while smirking to myself, *maybe all those stupid conversations with those train idiots weren't so fruitless after all*. And in parallel I was reminiscing about an old partner who couldn't pack appropriately for holidays where separate small overnight bags were required due to journeying over the course of more than one day before arriving at the long-term destination where only then larger suitcases would be practically accessible. I found myself chuckling as I walked beside these three companions across the black valley floor and noted that I should have taken her on more trips, particularly ones with slightly complex packing requirements. Meanwhile the banker was puffing on his pipe and humming to himself, with surprising and quite agreeable harmony. All was well, and all was calm, and though hysteria was surely waiting up ahead somehow, life seemed to make a wonderful sense for this untameable moment or two where only great notions seemed dare dance.

So to the mountaintops, we cheered, telepathically, *to the mountaintops!* Those cold and battered mountaintops swaying silent in the sky, beckoning wind and rain and storms of pain to break them down and make them feel. But the morning rays of sun, or evening ones, are surely far too golden and too full of hope to let any one of those snow-ridden peaks let slip and crumble down into this darkness that we dwell below. So yes, to the mountaintops; to the place where the sun last fades and freshly mounts assault each day, unless cloudy, and the place where we will be if we keep climbing till we can climb no more.

Take the path that winds, they said, *through dark fair-scented pine*, then on across a stream that runs from higher places, to meet with bare bold mountainside where the path shrinks small into submission but winds on still nonetheless. *It's a rocky path*, they said; a tricky one where boots will scuff and chink on rock and flint; where toes will tremble on high steps and knees will go unheard as they call us now to think of the way down and back again, and of the burden they will know. *Oh but who gives an ounce of care for a knee's lament when great skies soar above and we can almost touch them here and now?* We can be birds for just a moment now; great masters now of men; a prophet on a mount, that's basking in the light of God or even just a standard one; an astronomer astronomising stars and nightly things; or a mountain shepherd perhaps, watching sleep his sheep, or not — it may be they just stood there still — but either way he knew more peace in a world that he made small, than us, from our lowlands where coin grumbles and grates on minds that pale and burn and rue the day we sought for more than a breeze across a mountainside, a raindrop on a canopy, or some old browned autumn leaves that are crunching brightly underfoot.

And on, past wild goats that crackle freely over crumbling cliffs above to scatter earth and stone and send it sprinkling down below in their wake and their traversing of great heights with no false foot or clumsy stumble that we mere pretenders might fall foul to in this foreign mountain land. Below the gliding eagle there who's riding bits of air that we could never see yet we could suppose were relatively warm and did facilitate the conquering of high and mighty ridges. And this we'll point and sigh in awe at because we think it so majestic and magnificent, because it's big and bold, and because it simply just looks good. And if it calls out as it rides across those ridges, we'll awe even harder and sigh even louder, because that would be even gooder. How those dark wings would block out the sun.

Oh, watch out for that rock! one of us might call, as we pass below some crackling cliff of troublesome old goats; perhaps we'll take shelter, in a small cave, or just a less satisfactory overhang barely big enough for us all. We could eat our sandwiches there, yes, and look across the path we'd come and think so full of satisfaction, *look how far we've come, yes, we must be good, we are doing good work here — a good day's work.* And then we'll move on and up, smiling to ourselves with some sort of wry, knowing that we're perhaps nearly there, perhaps nearly found, where the sun first greets the world and says its last farewells, unless cloudy, and where we'll be when we can climb no more.

So it was in this vein, spurred on by hearty telepathic cheering, that we commenced our grand offensive through these cowering hills. And in high spirits we marched on till dusk, till we'd done what surely must be a good day's work, and set up camp, light of heart, heavy of foot, and ready for a supper enhanced by taletelling and stargazing amidst the crackling flame of fire.

Some days later while still contesting the foothills of this great plateau, our camp woke to the sound of rustling and excited fidgeting.

"Hey, listen here!" the banker whispered eagerly while rustling about an old map he seemed to have procured from his excessive array of things, "I've been told there's a mysterious place near here we can find, with beauty and tranquillity that washes all worries and thought from mind!"

"And who told you that?" D asked, looking sceptically at the figure who looked rounder and more little than usual.

"The train guard — he was quite sure on the matter!"

"Yeah, he says lots of things and he hardly seems real," D continued, "not even sure what he does most of the time he's meant to be train guarding or whatever."

"Well," the banker bartered on, "he's marked a place on this old map he gave me and the map looks real, and old, and mystical enough!"

So after some murmured and doubtful debate, we fastened up our laces, tightened up our belts, shuffled on our ruckies, mentally prepared to various extents, and drawing courage from the clinking sound of water bottle readying, set off from camp into this jungle that we'd hesitantly agreed was full of ancient treasures and mystical places. The banker was really excited and he ran off in front into the trees, compass in hand. We caught up with him a few minutes later, tangled up in some vines, and he'd lost the compass. But some wonderful sounds came to ear to dampen this dark detail as we crashed through the tricky mess of tree and vegetation; varieties of bird they were presumably, calling out over the treetops and bringing vibrancy to a twisted place that would otherwise feel amiss. So we marched on in column formation quite confidently, like a posse of Victorian explorers on their way to Eldorado and the tranquillity they'd been promised. We had our old map, we had the little stone path underfoot to lead us safely through this sea of mysterious organicness, we had our supplies, including freshly-made sandwiches packed in lunchboxes with orange and chocolate accompaniments, and best of all we had our blind optimism which can never go unpacked when spearheading a great expedition into the unknown.

So on through tree and twisted vine until a well-awaited luncheon time when sandwiches might save the day by way of ham and cheese and bread in orderly format all held fast by spread, and when we could speak of ways and routes through which we might pass and had already passed, or through which we did pass presently. And though this matter might seem tiresome, a pertinence did demand it, for we were pioneering, and paths through wild were all our world. *Up now! Up!* and shouts of haste were issued then, our hearty sandwiches naught now but crumb on face; onwards was the matter of the afternoon, to delve forth and far into vast unknown at a befittingly unrelenting pace.

It was sometime later that the expedition had proven unsatisfactory, and to our dismay, because we'd pioneered so heartily and hard. The jungle path through the sea of mysteries had been long and quite repetitive; all the trees looked the same, plus the medley of bird song that would render this place amiss if absent was annoying because it all just sounded the same. In addition, we'd elected to utilise the majority of rucky capacity for sandwiches and books in the hope that we might enjoy some reading breaks. These had proved quite heavy and so we'd sacrificed water volume (Djako's recommendation based on rainforest natural rain supply concepts) as a seemingly reasonable solution to the quandary. But it hadn't rained and the water supply had rapidly diminished to naught.

"Yeah I think this is just a jungly forest," D said as we looked around at each other questioningly, "and not like a rainforest jungle, because it's quite cold and this region doesn't seem equatorial does it…"

"You know what guys," Djako said, looking optimistically to the sky while brushing off this statement and shushing us with a finger, "I reckon I can hear a stream…"

"No we're not doing that again," I quickly interjected, "not after the last time we encountered water-related challenges and engaged in hearing-assisted exploits."

"Let's push on through this bit of jungle." he went on to suggest, again brushing off valid-sounding statements with ease.

"Yes but how much is this *bit*?" the banker whimpered, "It could be a very big bit?"

"Nonsense, optimism is the answer in dire situations such as this," Djako announced loudly, before screaming and achieving a state of frenzy, "ADVAAAANCE!"

A few moments later we were entangled and blocked up in this *bit* of jungle. So we used our last resort and sent some flares up — flares plural because they kept getting stuck in the trees. After deciding no one was coming — who's out here anyway plus flares stuck in trees — we just pushed on until we barely could no more and we came upon a green light on a dark secluded plain sitting bare between the trees. And it was pulsing kind of gently but all around with no source that willed to show itself.

"Have we stumbled through to the treasure that's been

waiting us?!" the banker called through the throbbing light.

Though it felt more like we were being consumed in this place that did not seem fit for dreams or even torrid tales, because it weighed on us and confused now muddled minds with its strangeness and its inexplicable presence.

"No this is some ruse!" D shouted, "Plotting out foul fortune or some untoward trickery for poor lost souls like we!"

"TO THE GREEN LIGHT!" Djako called, his voice floating true over our dismay, "Straight to it now, and through — to the other side break through!"

And surprisingly inspired we found ourselves scampering lightly on across the strange bare land, through a final row of trees, then down a fearsome slope and out, to see clear again and finally break through the other side of this deep jungle where it felt good because we felt free like we did before; perhaps this could be the mysterious tranquillity we'd been promised by the treasure map. We looked across the new plain below, a proper one this time, with only golden light now pulsing, although it wasn't actually pulsing, only gently basking grassland beneath the setting sun. And lazy rivers wound upon the plain to give it glinting royal causeways. And here we wondered if this was where the mist settles, in this place beyond the mountaintops then leafy oaks and pine.

"Is this where the mist settles?" Djako murmured as we stared across the great plain.

"What do you mean?" D asked as inquisitive faces turned to look at Djako.

"I don't know," he replied, "it just feels like this is where the mist would gladly settle on a crisp morning to have the sun shine above it and make this plain seem magic from the precipice we stand on here."

And so surprised by the softness of thought that now came from this crude creature, we pondered on a settling of the mist a while.

"Either way," Djako continued dreamily, "when the mist is settled, and the moon risen, and the bay of a wolf drifts across the cold air, we could look up to the sky, and see stars, or just god, but not one that man ever imagined. This precipice could be a place where it all ends, or maybe all begins; whichever one, we could smile to ourselves perhaps, knowing that we got somewhere, or were about to know something new…"

"Right…" the banker said, putting a stop to the dreaming and regarding, "shall we go back in and give finding it another go?"

"Finding what?" I asked, more dreamily than I'd have liked while still looking curiously at Djako.

"The treasure stuff from the treasure map." he snapped back.

"Oh yeah…"

"No, let's push on down to this lavish plain!" D cried triumphantly, perhaps inspired by Djako's soft words, because he sounded like him now while cutting through our quiet conversing, "We've broken free of this beastly place at last!"

"But we've left half our stuff at camp." I replied while feeling regretful to be the bearer of such news.

"Oh yeah, right… we'll have to go back through then."

So we sighed and gave the plain one last look, before

171

starting off back through, dreading the green light, the water situation, the food situation, the trees because they were all the same, the birds because they would not stop from singing, the incoming commentary from certain posse members, the general minds of other posse members, and also our own minds, not least because they were potentially making things up, like green light that doesn't even exist. So though we started off back through, we did not do so feeling well.

12

THE CONCLUDING OF THE jungle expedition saw a period
spent recuperating/arguing upon arriving back to a camp
that felt desolate and disheartened, and we perhaps came
close to surrender for a time. Though with a newfound grim
resolve come by the breaking of next morning, we shuffled
on our ruckies for what felt the umpteenth time, buckled up
loose waist straps, and even fastened too the little neck ones
that don't do anything; but we were feeling kind of cavalier,
so no amount of pointlessness could restrain or haunt us
now. And then we looked across the land, our defiance
simply brimming, to where we would now venture; where
ranging high and low we took these hills by storm, and they
could offer no resistance as they reeled on in surprise, shaking from the sheer resilience of battered old hope that was
more relentless than anything nature could dream muster.
We just kept walking on, marauding at will, a little wiser

perhaps, for days, when no thoughts seemed come to mind. But thoughts weren't needed, and probably weren't even recommended; we were just ranging high and low now, hearts blazing through the mirk, and savouring the reeling of these hills. We could feel them shaking beneath the pounding of each boot that championed a sure foot that would not waver. And the sun shone, or clouds came, sometimes to rain and sometimes just to roll across the sky that always was above us. But our minds were indifferent; impregnable to such inconsequential series of events that would not destabilise us now.

Was it indifferent to us, the sky? I started thinking though, when thoughts came creeping back to pry, *or without a working mind was even indifference an impossibility?* I decided it might have been indifferent to us since no empathy came from its depths, even for all its beauty; and yet it chose to exist through some kind of working mind, even if it always had been and always might be some law of physics or another god we made up one day.

"Why are you always so discontent in your relationships?" Djako shouted over at me, cutting through the stillness and tearing things back to reality.

"What — w-what are you saying?" I found myself spluttering as I fumbled for words and reeled in surprise, already destabilised enough from notions of physics and gods, and feeling now an empathy for these shaking hills, due to the reeling.

"Yeah, don't try and sneak around the subject this time," he continued, "you always get scared and decide they're not the one."

"Well yeah I lost my belief in the one when someone stole my one, questioned my unquestionable love, and never gave it back!"

"Ha, who stole it then?" D laughed.

"Well, my mind slash self did." I replied, "...Slash the world, yeah the world in general stole it, because the world's indifferent and if you ever thought it cared you should have a rethink and realise it just does random shit!"

"Ha, excellent attitude!" D laughed again, frolicking in this sudden eruption of strained dialogue.

"And you can't just say it was because they lacked basic duvet skills." Djako added.

"That was *one* time I said that!" I hastily pointed out, "And it was only ever one possible reason why it didn't work out. There was loads of possible reasons — loads. *Were* — *were* loads."

So plagued now by the ghastly return of thoughts — just standard ones — with sleeves up-rolled, we took a seat, and took again, to pensivity, or maybe to the absence thereof, depending on what counts as pensivity. And this lasted a while. There was the sound of the banker puffing and mupping on his pipe — *mhhup mhhup mhhup... phffff...* and so on. It was calming and brought some solace to mind. Birds and their songs came and went. Leaves and breeze met to rustle then grow quiet and alone again. Behind me knew an intermittent clinking where D flicked small stones that bounced on tinny rock before coming to rest on new horizons. Meanwhile, Djako had announced he was going hunting sometime before and still hadn't returned to make any of his important-sounding announcements. So I lay in the sun then and thought how good it was.

I woke a while later from dreams of escape, and stillness, and great horizons, to find Djako had returned.

"Oh hello," I said, remarking his empty-handedness, "what did you catch?"

"Just a reconnaissance exercise." he replied.

"Right, but you said you were going hunting…"

"Nah, just a reconnaissance exercise."

I looked at the back of his head for a while as he arranged himself happily into a comfy napping position, then in order to finish off the afternoon siesta in peace, I decided to get back to dreams and less disturbing horizons.

And I'd been right to do so, because upon waking not long later as the sun was going down, disturbing horizons were persisting. To my disappointment, as I leisurely strolled the camp and did a few stretches, the banker reminded me it was my turn to light the fire and get dinner going with Djako that night. But he hadn't caught anything for dinner had he.

"What are we gonna cook then?" I snapped at him, as I imagined all the supplementary stretching and strolling I might be missing out on, "And this firewood you've collected's all damp!"

I threw the wood down and scowled at him a bit but he didn't seem to notice.

"The banker's promised something better," he replied as he started singing some horrible song and bent over a pile of firewood he was tending to, "and this wood just needs some fine care and lovin'."

"Rigghhhtt, what's for dinner?" D said, rubbing his hands and looking optimistically round as he came to join us by the crackling fire we found ourselves surrounding now the night had settled in, "What did he catch for us?"

"He didn't catch shit," I said, "he just walked about the woods."

"I'm sure he tried." the banker interjected with a tone of reprimand.

"Right." I muttered, looking darkly over at Djako who was deciding not to join in the current conversation as he didn't like the topic.

So we just continued to roast some weird nuts the banker had found over the fire.

"Some girolles to accompany these crunchy little delights would be lovely right now." the banker said.

"What are they?" D asked.

"They're a particularly tasty variety of mushroom that's found in the wild — too difficult to cultivate domestically."

"I always thought it's not worth the risk picking mushrooms," I murmured as I regarded one of these nuts that we'd been subjected to, "they could be poisonous couldn't they."

"Nooo, nah," the banker replied with a wave of his hand, "girolles are very distinctive — only a small child or sheer amateur could mix them up for another."

"Oh," I said, "well maybe this type is an exception then…"

And we continued riveting fireside discussions for a while, before discovering that silent stargazing and private dreaming was just as good.

For the next few days we pushed on, and it came to our attention that this plateau we'd been traversing was all that a great plateau should be. It stood fashioned of pine and rock and hill, with lost valleys in between, each of which must have harboured little worlds of their own. And fresh rivers cut it, breaking it down into manageable pieces of land, fit for entities such as ours. We could traverse one in a day, or less, and feel good at the end for we'd entered a new piece, or two, and so we'd surely progressed. While some pieces were calm, soft, homely woods of oak and birch or whatever other tree they were, some were steep and treacherous wrought with cliff and windswept forest, and some of course were unknowable for they were too impenetrable and grandiose, too high and lost for mere humans to fathom frequenting. But the mountains, these majestic peaks, that watched serenely over all, would not stop to ask in silence who might dare to challenge them; who might sprawl out from hiding in amongst these gentle foothills, these perfumed woods of wise old oak, to meet their rocky barren slopes. These pretenders would stand through steel wind and snow and sun, and would not waver, but watch with stillness always, to remind us that we were only small things that cannot but wander and endure through the greatness. So we knuckled down, with heads down too, and picked through this great plateau, praying half and hoping, we not be swallowed up just yet.

We came to make camp one fair evening later as the knuckling down and picking through was fully underway and bearing not bad fruits it seemed; the commanding ridge we'd come upon overlooked a mighty delta that stretched away below and glistened in the setting sun as far the eye could see. And so for our camp this royal spot was chosen, *well befitting of our way*, we felt, as we nodded to each other and gladly claimed the place as ours. I took up my position on a tussocky knoll where Djako decided he too would pass the night even though I'd looked at him incredulously as he came to establish himself in what had clearly been my area. Anyway, we made the most of it and looked out onto the kingdom below.

"Hey throw me that will you?" I called over.

Djako clanked the steel water flask shut and threw it over to me. I unclanked the flask and took a sip. It wasn't actually water mind you; it was squash, orange squash, and I'd never really liked squash. I liked juice, and water was fine, but an in between was never necessary. Squash is an in between and Djako said he liked it, and so all water had to be contaminated with squash. So I sipped the squash as the last of the sun's rays fell upon my face, and looking at the magnificent shining delta below, squash flask in hand, I wondered how it had come to this.

I woke the next morning gazing into blue sky and chose to wonder a while more before grinding mind into a state of sufficient action/alertness required to permit a functioning that could hope to challenge the assault of a brand-new day.

"Not a cloud in the sky!" Djako called from not far off, "Mmmm, fresh morning air never ceases to thrill!"

I saw my breath on the cold air and enjoyed it as the functioning rolled into place, and in this way, the day had begun.

"Get the bacon aaaaan!" D cheered from somewhere down below, "Get it aaan!"

There seemed an air of optimism in the camp this day; *it must have rolled down from these wild high hills somehow,* I reckoned to myself as the smell of bacon sizzling on a campfire came to join the view I'd woken to. I thought I'd been hearing pots and cooking utensils clanking below, and so this conjecture was confirmed. I imagined the banker pottering attentively around his stove, murmuring to himself, eager to prepare things correctly, and I took a moment to enjoy the image before scuffling down the little knoll we'd been occupying for squash/sleep consumption, to witness the scene firsthand and compare the imagined version to the non-imagined one.

So sizzling bacon came to melange with rubbing hands, stamping feet, and steaming coffee amongst other satisfactory things. This was a good morning as optimism, and that of a sustained nature which did make it of interest, was indeed in the air. And though it was cold as can be with a frost nipping through us, it was cosy yet, for we and the way of things willed it so.

"Today I'd like to talk about conviction." the banker said as we sat and soaked up the comfort that this morning had chosen grant us.

"Conviction!?" D cynically exclaimed, "Forgot that existed."

"Conviction will always exist for those who know where to find it." he continued firmly.

"Haha! You sound like you're from an epic tale — there's no epic tales around here, friend."

"Don't be so sure that you know what epic is or isn't! Life is epic and there's no heroes needed here — just long and arduous, or short and simple suffices — no titles or songs of bards. Our lives are epic and you should know that!"

With that, the banker threw down his breakfast crockery, a little more wildly than he'd perhaps have liked, but, presumably with no less conviction, and mildly brandishing the stick he walked with, he quietly huffed and puffed away up the knoll to look across the land — maybe in an epic way, although it didn't seem that epic. But, you know, we didn't mention it and just sat a while longer as time trudged on in a uniform manner until broken by a cold flow of air that came down yonder from some higher place; *from these deceitful wild high hills*, I muttered to myself as the sense of optimism and comfort silently sounded its retreat, leaving in its place a sense that wasn't known and had no will to be. And this made it a disconcerting sense; a sense we'd rather not have succumbed to. But the succumbing was done and so accepted with pained hearts since to resist would only have been venturing still further into dissonance.

"The best thing to do, in states of dissonance like this chaps," the banker called as he observed the sky around us and descended from his lone position on the grassy knoll, "is to pick up your packs and don't stop walking till the sun's on your back and you know you've done good today!"

Well the sun is on our backs now, and I liked to think we

knew we'd done good today. For the plateau had been traversed, and so new sections now waited up ahead, while old were laid to memory, to be reflected thereupon, romanticised about maybe, missed to varying extents, or gladly left forgotten. Either way, this plateau was under heavy assault, and it would slowly crumble away beneath our feet until we would surely reach the stars and understand something new.

"We're gonna look at the stars tonight," Djako blurted out as we finalised our camp, "and we're not gonna stop until we find some answers!"

"What kind of answers?" D demanded looking pretty blasé.

"Any kind of answers — any kind of answers will do."

"Yeah and it doesn't matter if they're good or bad ones!" the banker cheered, "It makes no difference, because who decided they were bad or good anyway?"

"Yeaaahhh!" we all cheered back with a spark of fervour as the motivational speaking overcame us and made redundant any actual meaning of words or propositions.

So we took up camp on this eve of resolve and hunkered down for a long night. Because a long night it would be when we'd see flash and flicker of starry light above, and when unfazed we would retaliate in worthy style with flame of heart and flicker of thought or dream that would skitter and scamper to scorch this cold night with the hope of man. It would be just the sky and us and it would be a gaze until the death, i.e. sleep for us or morning for the sky, when the victor would come out all enlightened.

Well the battle is lost isn't it, I muttered to myself as I felt myself awaken, for sleep had come before the morning chorus had had cause to break the day, and so the stars did die after us that night, perhaps with a wry smile, as the answers they held and the majesty they knew would be safe and sound and taken with them to a grave beyond the sun. I lay and hoped then, that the stars would rain down one day, and bury this pain, if it was even pain. And what's wrong with pain anyway.

"...Or bury this plateau that doesn't even seem that great anymore, in fact it seems pretty boring now, yeah, no majesty — where's the majesty gone..."

"WHAT'S THAT!?" Djako shouted at me as I realised I'd been mumbling out loud.

"Imagine a world where pain and frustration et cetera, was just as good as pleasure and satisfaction," I replied nonchalantly to brush off this malfunctioning of thought through murmur as we swung our ruckies on, "wouldn't that be simpler?"

"Right," he answered, "but pain and frustration is hardly very nice..."

"Yeah but why not?"

"Well, it just doesn't feel nice, and all this pain and sadness and frustration business makes you feel like you're losing in life somehow."

"OK so if we said it was good and a sign of succeeding, it would be alright then?"

"OH COME ON!" D loudly interrupted, "Do we have to have this conversation again? You do realise we've done it already, and loads of times, just in slightly different formats!"

"Sadness and these related things are like the silent sisters of happiness," the banker intervened, "often discarded and overlooked, but without them, this happiness would just be a husk, and laughter would become an infernal reverberation throughout the void."

"Yeah, pretty good summary." I said, pleased with the surprising show of potential support, "So you're saying pain's not so bad right?"

"...So embrace these things — and walk as one towards the stars," the banker continued, kind of ignoring me actually, "while we watch in peace even as our dreams do break around us, happiness and related things on one shoulder and pain et cetera on the oth—"

"Haha WHAT!" D laughed to cut him short, "Have you been rehearsing this? Since when do you talk about concepts and stuff in this stupid dramatic way?"

Yeah, I thought to myself, *he kind of killed it.*

"I talk about lots of things!" the banker snapped back, "You've just got attention problems!"

And he strode off, leaving D, and us if even be it just collaterally, in his wake. *Hmmm, although maybe I do sometimes too...* I returned to thinking doubtfully as I watched the little fat man huff and puff determinedly ahead and reflected on his killing it.

I saw the sun rise some days later as we continued to battle this less impressive piece of plateau that had seemed bland and incomplete. And I chose to sit and watch, to feel the world wake with it, connecting a while to something complete. And everything was innocent when the beams of gold crept up over the edge of the earth and shined with no purpose, and the world rose and reacted for no reason. But as I turned to see the others smugly sleeping, I started wondering why I'd been put on breakfast duty that morning — I was sure I did it yesterday — and so the moment was lost, and the connection broken, since incompleteness seemed to grow again, even if against my will.

And so what had to be important about this supposedly incomplete piece of plateau, I came to deliberate as we forged and picked on through, was its *lack* of majesty; boasting no great ridgeline or bold mountain peak, nor view across the world. So that one might lend a care to draw from passing detail, like a fallen chestnut resting now, in amongst a bed of leaves; *hello you, I hope you grow one day… or feed a hungry squirrel perhaps…*. And then one might look up, or stoop to spot a deer treading softly through the trees; ferreting out fine pastures where it might frolic in the sun a while and nibble fresh green grass. And though such green grass might prove disappointingly pauce in this sub-fine pasture it did happen upon, here the deer would linger for a short time even so, before retreating home as the night set in; and yes it would do so in a slightly disappointed fashion, due to the paucity, but it would do so nonetheless, and the world would be the same. And meanwhile we'd put an end to our unseemly spectatorship, for this was no zoo, and, succumbing to a wry smile, just a passing one but enough to warm the heart, we'd forge ahead again bearing ever more fervour, knowing that majesty was just majesty.

13

*C*RUNCH, CRUNCH, CRUNCH *crunch crunch crunch.*

What was about to happen sounded like some kind of one-movement orchestral work comprising rhythms not so dissimilar to those of a Spanish 3/4 dance form, assuming the work had nothing but natural objects in the wild and a troop of four great explorers to bolster its orchestral armoury. And while one defeatist might have predicted that nature's orchestra would refuse to play it, we did crunch on nonetheless, playing it.

Crunch, crunch, crunch crunch crunch crunch.

The sound of eight feet came together, quite unwittingly, into time, upon the gravelly unsuspecting path we found ourselves parading now. We'd come to enter a gorge that felt like some imperial walkway to a royal palace that awaited us on the other side. And somehow an overwhelming sense of triumph came upon us as we began our march on through, which expressed itself eloquently via our un-suspecting selves. Initially noticing the irresistible beat, I came in with a pair of small slates and the music of our feet was henceforth recognised, appreciated, and elaborated upon.

Crunch, crunch, chacka-dee-chack chacka-dee crunch crunch.

After several rounds of this, D entered the movement with a wonderful *ting ting* created using some of his metallic crockery.

Crunch, crunch, chacka-dee-chack chacka-dee ting ting.

By this point we were all smiling triumphantly to our-selves, and to each other even too as our eyes caught and sparkled in delight, revelling in our discovery and im-promptu musical development that was emerging in this once-standard stone passage which now probed the fron-tiers of the realm of fantasy.

BahhummmmmmbAH! BahhummmmmmbAH!

Djako had dropped in, playing with, and gliding effort-lessly between, the frontiers of bass and tenor. Only the banker remained, and what unfathomed heights marked the majestic moment he began as the mimicked sound of an oboe sprang and then danced from his lips, providing the marvellous melody our beat was worthy of and had been readily waiting for. And it was all crescendoing and rever-berating and bounding off those stunned stone walls of gorge, trembling from such incontestable assault, and we were lost from ourselves for a fine passing moment as our spectacle graced this disregarded little valley somewhere up in the mountains, where the sound of a foot or the ting of some metal crockery would perhaps never be heard again, and perhaps indeed had never been.

So we marched on in triumph along this narrow acquiescing pathway, and the world seemed right; it seemed the dark drapes that swirled in mind to cloud and misguide were no more. *For this was the only way,* we came to theorise; *there was no other way;* this would lead us true, straight through rock and crumbled stone, where dead desire and broken dream would become alive and all unbroken. No look hither, right left or even thither, nay, no glancing a bit round, a little up or sort of slightly down; the way was true, this way was one, and at last our desire had come to join us, settled now at peace in the palm of each our hands that cared to shake no more. *Sound the trumpets!* we proposed, *for goodness heaven's sake*, and then well jolly did, even if inside our heads except for one who tried do it with his hands and mouth out loud to nearly massacre the moment, anyway, *we march on!* we fiercely cheered, telepathically, *these damn syndromes of destiny lie in tatters now, and freedom calls; it's beyond the ridge there, look! It's been waiting for us there.*

Well, it was several hours later and we'd decided to stop the noise since it had become tiresome as had the gorge which was still proceeding with itself, while triumph had proved transient. This innocent little passage that had started out as the facilitator of our magical musical mystery tour was to become something of ours that offered a gradual asphyxiation (mental mostly, possibly physical depending on whether we imagined it or not) along with a poor view —

kind of reminiscent of the jungle actually, which got us nervous due to memories, their recent nature disallowing nostalgic trickery to have settled in just yet. And then it was hot in the gorge even though it was cold and clearly snowing. And we couldn't breathe and just talking was difficult and nothing meant anything; what did it matter where any of us came from, what we all thought, what we each claimed gave us meaning in life, or why Mozart was better than Beethoven but not Ravel, and who the hell gives a shit about Austerlitz or strategy or even that ridiculous Rorke's Drift. Every word was heavy, each sentence a far cry to finish; not just mentally, but physically for the mouth and tongue too. All attempt at amicable fine-flowing conversation fell foul and felt false just as soon as worn-out words came forth, awkwardly heaving out one's mouth. And each time we'd strike again with various desperate arrays of words, they did naught but wane, bringing all that felt heavy and meaningless to a culmination; to a pedestal that towered in the bareness at which we could only gaze upon in horror. This was akin to some kind of melting of mind with all blissful joy, deep sadness, or great gallant fervour — from which dreams of beauty and passion are born to hold life at its prime and most poignant — melting and crumbling away through outstretched arms of desperation. With all the power of the beautiful human mind to stop them fading, yet with no power at all; nothing but useless, hopeless anguish reaching out from somewhere you thought was surely gone and guarded in a tomb you'd resealed too many times to tell after opening it one day when growing up had come upon you. And finally, and even worse, a numbness seemed here reign, because by the end I'm not sure we even did despair.

In addition to mental complications, our gorge didn't seem to be on the map we'd been given and while it must have been going somewhere, this somewhere was unknown to us. But what could we do but continue along the lonely way which gave no answers and showed no face, while empathy was only to be found in each other which, at least, provided some comfort and acted as our little light in the mirk that seemed to silently swirl and cling, only lifting for some hopeful moment before falling back, having failed to find liberation or some purpose other than the swirling and the clinging. As we continued, we were aware we might have been becoming a little delirious although it was pretty hard to say. D was murmuring increasingly to himself with strong notes of dissatisfaction, matching those that the banker now incessantly hummed, no longer supporting the great harmonies that had once come. Djako tried, on numerous occasions, to offer some kind of inspirational speech which held all the hallmarks of Americanesque optimism; the lack of subtlety proved difficult to bear though and only appeared to increase the intensity of the murmuring and the humming. I myself tried numerous techniques to guard my composure, including living the present moment, accepting the situation and appreciating all, etc. The mental shutdown required to effectively implement these flagrant techniques came best when asleep though and so I usually found I had to wait until bedtime to enjoy their fruits.

There were still great days though, that reminded us it

wasn't all so hopeless and without wonder, like little lapses in consciousness and water bottle drama.

"It looks like that water bottle's gonna fall out." I called up to D who marched ahead one morning.

"Nah it's not." he shouted back.

"It definitely looks like it's gonna fall out." Djako agreed.

"Nah it's not, that's just how it sits, I always keep it like that."

"Why don't you just adjust it slightly," the banker suggested, "to be on the safe side."

"Nah, no point."

A few miles later it turned out it had fallen out so then we didn't have enough water and got dehydrated for a while.

"Should have adjusted it." I said to him.

"Yeah," he mumbled back disappointedly, "I probably should've."

That was a good day, bordering on great.

And then there was this evening when we became aware that the moon was looking down on us, replacing our day's light of gold with that of silvers and of shadows and of new noises come to pulse around us; pale timid calls, and those of sorrow, and some that reminded us we were only small beings in a world that could still hide and too know us better than we did ourselves, even for all our books and buildings and tools that gave comfort to a race of minds that couldn't even do a gorge. So this was a good day also, maybe a great one, because we were left wondering and while smiling too.

Some walking later we came upon a lone tree growing in the middle of the gravelly path. Its base was smooth and glistening with fresh dew and it looked young and full of hope. But as you followed its path to the sky, it became bent and twisted, with arrays of desperate arms reaching out and then drooping dry and withered back towards the black earth it grew from that had promised it so much. Some determined branches had grown into the sides of the gorge and cemented themselves within the small crevices that ran through the jagged rock; almost as if to hold this tree up and prevent it from collapsing on itself. Some branches were still growing upwards, and though surrounded by broken arms that had lost themselves some time before, they kept hope nonetheless. For no reason, this hope — perhaps just that to grow is a hopeful thing and can make an empty gorge or no matter where, a where which wasn't empty, from which memories might be remembered.

"Nice tree." D said, as we marched on by.

And I smiled at leisure, even sporting a satisfied pout, as I noted how right he was.

That evening, as we crunched on, when the tree and the pouting was just memory and as all seemed to be getting just too hopeless and too lost, a little wooden door appeared in the side of the rocky gorge. A sign lit by a lamp that swung creaking above it read *The Gorgeous*. We all agreed this was a very clever name, even if a little mocking, and the warm glow the lamp produced that worked its way through the gloom was all too charming to pass by unaddressed. So we went straight in, and like a drink in a cosy pub adorned by the light of a crackling fire after a winter's day walk in the country, we sat down for a drink, retreated now from the cold, and found ourselves lit by the light of a crackling fire in this place we could only describe as a pub. It was fantastic. Strange, we had to admit, as it was hard to imagine anyone else had ever been here, making the economic viability of a pub questionable or just downright hopeful, while several other questions lurked here and there which were quickly forgotten and brushed aside as quite unjustified once the first few drinks were through; you know, like maybe it was only there to welcome weary lost souls on the off chance they did stumble there, which would make it a far greater pub than any one that stood for coin or things like viability.

The innkeeper was dressed in a hooded cloak and reminded us of someone that we couldn't put our finger on. We asked him some of our initial questions as we were seated but his response was usually just a chuckle or some cryptic reply which left the questioner with an answer of perceived high quality and a sense of appreciation but nothing much by way of clarity, which was often realised too late on to warrant re-asking the question. We watched his hood fall off at one point during the haze of the night and I exclaimed that it was our train guard, before the hood was quickly repositioned. The innkeeper said I was wrong, and the matter lay forgotten. *And who even cares*, I thought all nice and brazenly carefree.

A woman bearing all the hallmarks of beauty sat alone at a table in the corner, rolling an empty glass through her fingers, her deep eyes glassed over as she did. She looked at us but said nothing and for some reason neither did we. Perhaps nothing needed to be said; you could feel a sorrow, a feeling that the world had betrayed her even for all her beauty and innocence. And like a child who had dreamed and perhaps had happiness once, only a desperate daring determination to cling to something of hope remained. I thought I felt this energy the moment I saw her face and my eyes met with hers, and without explanation, the desire to embrace and know all there was to know of this fair spirit came calling from a deep place. But no great embrace would emerge to be realised; perhaps it was fear of disloyalty to those already in one's life, or a fear of something too pure and perfect that would bring one too close to the answers one searches for, and so prematurely ending the restlessness that gives some strange reason to go on. And so nothing would become of a connection that felt so right, found in the strangest of places. It was just a passing dream anyway; a wild idea based on naught. We'd be lost from each other forever after that night, without ever having said a word, and what could have been would never be, like some story from an epic tale with made-up creatures, dreams and monsters. At least it would be something though, to think about sometimes, when things were proving much too clear and plain, and hesitant pondering, could-have-beens, or far-off pining memory, had reached their limits of neglect.

"We've been stuck in this gorge for ages." I announced, gesturing at the innkeeper, to break the silent musing and realign the stumbling focus.

"Yeah and you're in charge of navigation and route planning!" Djako exclaimed, "Where's your famous planning now?"

"Well it's not on the map and so all we can do is keep going until the end." I pointed evidently out, "How are we meant to find the way when nothing of real value is on the map that idiot train guy gave us?!"

"You could just climb out of the gorge," the innkeeper suggested, "there's a place not far off, back from where you've come I'd say — it's not so hard to climb out that way."

This suggestion seemed all too obvious and easy and so we bent our minds together to collaborate and corroborate.

"Why've we never thought to climb out the gorge?" D muttered.

"Well," the banker meekly replied, "we'd assumed it was just too deep and difficult hadn't we..."

"Yeah I'm surprised *you* didn't think of climbing out," I said looking accusingly at Djako who was hanging his head now, "with your optimism."

"Or perhaps you were scared of leaving." the innkeeper called over, "As while it was seemingly your jailor, it gave you security and a way that was only one and easy..."

"Right," I said, brushing his annoying lessons off, "and will climbing out lead us to the train tracks then?"

"There's no trains round here." he bluntly replied.

We scrambled to check the map again, and had to admit, with great reluctance, that while there was some black line running along the far side, there was no key which might confirm that a train track was indeed that which it repre-sented.

"So why did you think it was a train track?!" Djako cried.

"Intuition." the banker snapped back quick, but even then, a look of perplexion rising on his features, like losing faith in his conviction, "…Logical presumption."

"NO!" I shouted at him, "You said the train guard said it was, just like with your stupid jungle treasure map!"

"You know," D interrupted, "I'm not sure he did say the train guard said it."

"Anyway what can it be then?" I demanded.

"Could just be a small path," D suggested, "or a cliff where it all ends."

"Great so we've been following this map the whole time to a feature that doesn't even exist?!" Djako blurted out, "Or even worse, to where it all ends?!"

"Where are we gonna go now then?" I wondered out loud as bewilderment seemed settle in.

"We'll lower the map and climb." the banker muttered with resolved determination, which proved a timely change in tone that helped us all restabilise.

So the map was tossed away, thrown with censure to the ground, upon which a certain sense of liberation came to saturate the air around us that suddenly felt lighter.

With that we turned around, came back on ourselves, and marched forth the way we'd come, through the night by now, in search of this secret passage out the gorge. Before long, we came upon the tree we'd passed without too much thought, but with some degree of smiling not so long ago. It came into view, all lighted by the moonlight, all beautiful and twisted and bent and broken, and shrouded in a shining mist. Like maybe some fairies lived there.

"Do you think fairies live here?" Djako dreamily awed.

No one bothered replying.

"You know, these trees keep growing until they die," the banker said, "wondrous things."

"Don't all things keep growing till they die?" D asked sceptically.

We looked at it and wondered if all things kept growing till they die, and why it kept growing, losing sense of direction, gnarling at old wounds, yet finding new territory in the world, knowing new things, and pushing to what could only be demise.

"What do we do now?" D said, "It's blocking the path again."

We reflected. And then we continued to scrabble around it, to edge and squeeze our way through.

"Hey, let's climb up it!" Djako called as I squeezed around with D while the banker still spectated from behind.

We turned and saw him plant a foot, and it looked triumphant, so we did too. Then we grippled and grappled until we conquered the climb with a great display of bravery although it wasn't that far. Until we were out of this beautiful forsaken gorge atop this wondrous withering tree, where we saw the rising sun, sleepy clouds serenely milling in the valleys far below, glistening waterfalls here and there plunging silent distant heights, and it was all crusted in gold, or something like divine.

14

We woke later that morning to find ourselves encamped, in a pretty informal way admittedly, by a faint path up above the gorge. We agreed we'd probably trooped on a bit from the old treetop and then fallen asleep on this stony ground that must have looked comfy. We also decided the pub man had given us too much late-night whisky and we muttered how irresponsible it was before choosing a direction and walking on. And as things from the night before started becoming less and less cloudy, we decided furthermore that it was pretty irresponsible of the banker to have thrown down our map in contempt, even if it did feel liberating for a time. Because now we didn't know where to go and so seemed to be choosing directions at random. Djako said something about using the sun to navigate but this was completely irrelevant because he didn't know how to do it, and we didn't know which general direction we wanted to go in anyway.

"I thought we were going kind of west," Djako said in an attempt to defend his useless sun commentary, "so we could just continue in that general direction couldn't we?"

"Yeah but that was when the train tracks were there wasn't it," I answered, "but it turns out they weren't train tracks — we need paths now, we need features and stuff…"

"So we need something to aim for." D said.

"Yeh — features!" I replied while pointing at the banker, "But he's thrown our map away!"

"Hey! You didn't seem to protest much last night when I did so," he tried to reason back, "and you could have just picked it up instead of marching out the pub while going on about having claimed victory!"

"No, it's all your talk of conviction!" I replied, getting quite heated by now, "Tricking us into believing doing things like throwing maps away was a good idea, just because you did it with conviction and it looked good at the time — way over the wrong side of the line — blind idiocy slash optimism, not C and C at all!"

"What's C and C?" D interjected.

"Confidence and conviction!" I snapped back impatiently, brushing away his stupid questioning and walking on ahead, though more haughtily than I'd anticipated, which I was privately a bit disappointed about.

A while later, the morning was gladly consigned to history, because we'd had headaches and couldn't walk with the bravour we would have liked, and also because we'd had to suffer numerous realisations of how things done the night before weren't as good as they'd seemed before, and this had sapped morale. So morning done, things looking up, and the way ahead all faint and blurry, we thought it might be a good time to pick a spot for lunch. And not long later, we found a sheltered picnic spot, to guard us from the drizzle of this generally underperforming day.

Going into meditative mode because there was little other choice, I looked at the weathered stone we'd lunch beneath, the cracked bark of nearby tree, and then a feather fall, one of those small fluffy ones, lost now from its bearer and swirling on to find its own dear future. It came to rest in the mud for then, before my gaze passed on. And I thought how these might be our allies, all these simple things, persevering on the same side, together bearing all the beauty and savageness of the world, through the indifferent grasp of existence. Yes, the wall is manned, with such fair allies all around, and a little bit of comfort can perhaps be found, in the midst of this bare ground that we all share. *So we should just feel,* I prepared myself to turn and say, even while considering the risk of D saying we'd discussed it all before but in slightly different formats, *be the bearers of such privilege while disregarding any slipping into notions of how good it may or may not be. Yes,* I thought, *calmly watch the feeling, whatever shape or form it takes, so we might continue simply on our way that would surely feel ligh—*

"What are you doing slash being all quiet about?" Djako suddenly demanded.

"Whhhat?" I choked, rudely jolted from my pondering, "I'vvve just been trying to work things out. And I was about to say som—"

"Oh and did you?!" he shouted to cut me off.

"Well I thought I had done for a moment, but it's already going fuzzy."

I got up and banged my head on an overhanging piece of weathered stone.

"Fucking hell SHIT STONES!" I shouted as I squashed the fluffy feather into the mud. "Because you've cut me off haven't you! You cut me off!"

"...Right," the banker softly spoke up, "shall we get going?"

"Yeah..." I mumbled, before dragging heavy-feeling legs into motion so that they might bring resumption to a doubtful wandering on a while.

"Maybe we like climbing mountains just to see what's on the other side, and all around," I found myself saying a while later after things had calmed down, "you know, from a natural instinct perspective."

"Oh yeah?" the banker responded, with some encouraging sign of intrigue.

"Yeah, it would have always been useful, to see what's going on in our surroundings, discovering new routes, checking for places to explore and things like that."

"Yeah, reasonable hypothesis — I suppose with maps it's less useful now."

"Well yeah but I'm talking subconscious reasons." I replied, using willpower to ignore the nerve of his map comment considering recent map-related events while it had also just struck me that it was him that lost the compass in the jungle as well, making him responsible for the forfeiture of all navigational aids, "...You know, the reaction to the subconscious feeling that there's something we've not yet perceived — something we haven't yet discovered or mapped out. Plus our map doesn't seem to be that accurate, and you threw it away didn't you, along with the compass, so maybe it still is useful."

"Good point, good point." the banker concurred meekly, his map-throwing and compass guilt perhaps getting the better of him, but hopefully because he actually agreed as well.

"Haha," D laughed, "will you stop going on about mountains!?"

What an upsetting response, I thought. So I decided to stop going on about mountains and dispute with the low-quality audience instead.

"Right, what do you want to talk about then? Idiot."

But he just sighed in satisfaction and walked off smiling. *What an idiot*, I thought as I carried on behind him, and as I watched him up ahead, hoped he'd fall or twist his ankle a bit so that I could feel some secret satisfaction while pretending to sympathise, and know that he knew what was going on here, yet there was nothing he could do about it due to lack of proof.

Having retreated from converse with idiots, and managing to put aside plans of revenge, I thought how I longed to dream; not literal ones when sleeping, but just to consciously dream, or be in a dream. Of what, I didn't know; even for all I imagined, I couldn't know. But surely something of mystery marked by muffled sound echoing through a forgotten place where water gently lapped, under the grey-blue of a dusk sky and with a mist that silently crept over the corners of things and smelt of goodness; of wet smoky grassiness; a smell it must have taken from the rolling hills that surround us now as we stand on this little jetty on some shoreline of a silent lake or sea. And raw desire would beg regard it all, feel it and be of it all; make sure it be remembered, and savoured there to remedy a long-lost longing for something that had been or that maybe still could be; like being children under guard of mum and dad, on one summer holiday, by a lake or sea, with rolling hills all round, and when nothing could touch us now; even this cold creeping mist, as we were there invincible, love and innocence having made it so.

Though even in this dream, I'd see this warm hazy scene before me, and feel with all that I could muster, but know melancholy even then, since this would never suffice for it wouldn't be captured or really known and celebrated as well as it should have; I'd feel the scene already, slipping away through flailing fingers, doomed now to fall into naught but a nostalgic memory, lurking, and waiting to come to oneself here and there when the days would seem darker and more faded. And with it, it would bring a poignant twang of beauty and sorrow for time lived, and passed, and lost.

"Urghhhhh…" I found myself sighing, out loud apparently.

"What?" Djako asked.

"I dunno." I said, or possibly just thought, gazing out and running a pensive finger along my lip.

And with that we pushed on to the evening and great horizons that lay before us, trying to appreciate them as best we could even though it was basically impossible. Because it continued in this vein a while, waylaid always as we went, by thoughts and hard concepts, and tricky ideas that would not be routed, despite all rationale that we could rally. So yes, we got waylaid along our way, and we had only perseverance to bring us through each passing day that brought new trails and ponder.

It was later one night that we found our ears prey to a sound we agreed we'd all been privately dreading — a wolf's call, quite a lonely one, but they say they hunt in packs don't they, so maybe it wasn't that lonely.

"Maybe they'll go the other way?" Djako proposed.

"Oh… what a hopeful proposition." D answered, "You clown. We're going down!"

And yes, if anything, the rustle of nearby bushes and vegetation became all too evident to permit the toleration thereof in a manner that was light. Something had to be done, like, strategy, or implementation of theoretical anti-wolf techniques and stuff.

"Could we… perhaps make gunfire noises in order to

create the illusion that we're heavily armed and danger-
ous?" someone suggested — gingerly presumably — can't
remember who due to the stress, but probably Djako.

No one could think of a better idea, so we proceeded to
make an array of noises. The crashes seemed to be getting
closer though, while stress got contagious, and so we found
our noises evolving into ever louder panic-fuelled unidenti-
fiable sound. By the end we seemed to be just screaming
wildly, perhaps in the belief that death was upon us. But just
as these screams culminated and turned to last words, the
crashing seemed to ebb and die away again, leading to a
short pause; a tantalising one where eyes flickered between
one another in hopeful anticipation.

Well, nothing came, and so we congratulated ourselves
for our quick thinking and courageous actions/noises which
drove these wild beasts scampering in panic from our camp.
The extent of our self-congratulation was, pretty rife — going so far as to clap each other on the back while chuckling
amidst amused muttering and things like that. Then we
gladly took up sleeping positions in preparation for a peaceful night.

"Maybe it was just the wind..." D softly suggested a
while later as we were dozing off.

"What?" Djako shouted, choosing not to whisper.

"The noises in the trees and bushes."

"...Don't be ridiculous." the banker muttered to break a
short pause that had ensued for thinking.

I thought to myself that it *was* quite windy.

"It *was* quite windy..." Djako said.

The discussion ended here and so presumably we'd each

comfortably dozed off.

So with that, whether we were at peace or being ever pursued by an array of wild things, we couldn't be sure. But what difference did it make — there was only a pushing on to resume, whichever way round it was. Yet the waylaying felt a little lifted; a good deal remedied now; for we'd come a little close to death, permitting thoughts, ideas, and tricky things, to just feel good or hardly relevant for just a fleeting bit of time, before we'd forget again about the coming of the close.

We found ourselves climbing ever higher into this maze of mountain plateau, and the air was cold, and the days turned foggy and this train track that chose to elude us, or to simply not exist, was becoming a noticeable source of dissatisfaction, and morale amongst us seemed to be waning, even in that of the half-American, half-French, and half-whatever else — the one who defied maths itself. So our fellowship found itself coming to waver, as a fellowship must inevitably do where epic tales such as life are concerned, or so the banker would try claim. And this became a heated topic of debate as lunchtime was coming to a close.

"...But there's been no dragons or battalions of monsters in our lives." Djako replied as he swung his bulky rucky back on, "It's not been that epic yet, so, do we even need to falter?"

"Right," D scorned back, "and how often in real life are you actually going to be charging down hills fighting monsters and dragons and stuff?"

"We've got to have something to work towards," Djako started shouting, "a destiny, we've got to know who we are and who we'll come to be!"

"I rather think myself a gardener at heart." the banker softly interjected.

"Ha!" D laughed out, "What do you know about gardening?!"

"I know I'm at peace when I'm pottering around with my trowel and the bees are humming to and fro."

I wondered what I was then, what made me at peace, for it was not the work I did nor that which I might aspire to be. And so I wondered what I was. D too, had gone quiet, but he spoke up again then.

"There was a time when I... played piano, and I think I was at peace, for those moments. I guess I was a pianist."

"But no more?" I questioned.

"I don't know," he said, looking on wistfully, "I started trying to show more, want more from what I played. I wanted to create. And the songs were all there — they were there — I'm sure of it — I knew they were there in me, but I couldn't get to them — they wouldn't flow through my fingers how I'd want them to flow. And that which came wasn't pure — it didn't seem pure — it was higgle and piggle and pressurised squiggle; limp notes that stuttered under the pressure of expectation. And then I wasn't at peace anymore, when I played my piano — my fingers were cold and the magic was gone, and what did it even matter anyway. And now I'm no pianist no more."

It was one of his most candid outbursts I thought, and again I wondered what I was; perhaps even jealous now that these two were or had been something.

"You shouldn't give up you know," the banker said, "you could be a pianist again, when the time be ripe, and you're at peace again when you pause to play."

Maybe I'm a walker, I thought, *am I at peace when I'm walking? Or some kind of weird mountain being? How do you know when you're at peace? Hmmm....* I chuckled and wondered what Djako thought he was. But he'd gone quiet, and so I wondered whether he knew not either, what he was.

"Don't look down chaps," the banker chirped on, "if I knew who I was, or who I would come to be, then life might not be worth the wander!"

"I thought you were a gardener?" Djako pointed out.

"Yeah, but maybe I won't be next time I take up my trowel — the bees might be humming all out of tune!"

And then he climbed off down this nearby cliff, humming, but not out of tune, until he disappeared into the fog below, before so too did his fair song that resounded softly up to us on the cold silent air.

"...That was weird," D chuckled looking around at us incredulously, "the train's never down there!"

"Yeah, he's like a mountain goat." I said.

"What," Djako queried, "because he's wise?"

"No, because they can climb up and down steep slopes with relative ease."

"It's a shame he's gone though." Djako summarised as we prepared to push on, "We'll probably miss him, in a way."

We walked on a while before D broke the silence.

"I didn't know mountain goats were wise..."

208

"Yeah, that's owls." I said as we turned to look accusingly at Djako.

But he just walked on, probably having pretended not to hear us.

This grass is green, we thought as we finished the day and sat recuperating sometime later. It's greener than most we've known before. And rich. But one day it will brown and scorch in scathing sun that, though once warm and welcome, was no friend now and probably never was. And then this grass will crackle in flame, when Hell will be come, arrived in the nick of time, before the bells tolled and the angels came. Hmmm, yeah… it was too late, they came too late — waylaid by tricky concepts perhaps or other things like that — but whatever, this is no surprise is it; it always seems too late where time will be concerned…

"Hmmm, if only we could do away with things like time," I said, "it would all be so much more relaxing."

"This grass is green." Djako noted in response.

"Yeah, that's what we've just been saying," I retorted, scornfully so, looking round in disbelief, "that's what we've just been saying…"

So we sat a while longer on this green grass and thought in silence a while longer about greenness, and time and things. And then just listened as best we could, to the world.

"You know, I'm… not sure we were saying it." remarked D amidst the silence, "I think we were just thinking it…"

Oh shitting hell, I thought, and chose not to respond so that they might think I'd pretended not to hear, and that I sat still unencumbered by conflict and confusion.

"And anyway," I woke to announce the next morning, "how were we all just thinking it if we weren't saying it. Because then how would we have known to all be thinking the same thing?!"

But they were just grumbling responses or pretending not to hear.

"None of this makes any sense!" I continued shouting, "And I'm believing with less and less confidence anything that appears to be in this world!"

I looked over at D to see him strapping on his rucksack and dressed in some kind of running gear.

"What's going on?!" I incredulously demanded.

"I'm running to that ridgeline over there to see if the tracks are on the other side."

"But that's *miles* away!" I scoffed back.

"Yeah, and it's probably really difficult but I've got nothing else to do."

"You could just push up to the top with us?"

"Nah, no point, we need to find this train — I'll light a fire on the ridgeline if I find it, and you can come on over to join me."

And with that, he ran off, chinking on the stoney path he took. And then the chinking died away and I looked at Djako.

"What's going on?" I repeated, in no mood to play vocabulary, "Where's he gone and how were we all just thinking the same thing though?"

"Onwards." he replied with resolve and nodding reassuringly at me.

So I nodded back, thinking like I'd somehow missed something, but I was backtracking in my head, and no, I'd been there the whole time. Anyway, accepting what it was because there was nothing else to do, onwards we went.

For the next day or two we pushed on, looking across and gazing at this far-off ridgeline, waiting in hope for signs of D and the smoke of some fire, but none came. We thought we saw him once, with the binoculars he'd left us, but after further scrutiny it turned out it was just a mountain goat traversing a steep slope with relative ease.

15

THE MIST GENTLY swirled, ebbing here and there on nearby rock and remnants of broken old wall. Giving a world that was only damp green grass, grey stone, and the soft trudge of foot on field. So we might imagine where we may be.

It was a fresh mist; a welcoming one that wouldn't will to trick and lure poor souls as a cruel thick fog might. This was a grey guard; a wisp of shield that kept wandering minds safe and sound on solid ground, all insulated from tiresome things that ask to calculate and navigate. And when the harrowing pheasant's call came piercing through the fine crisp air, it did not seem so harrowing after all, for its lone lament awoke a wildness in heart that gave state of fret no quarter, while peace ran through the echoes of each cry, maybe as each never asked an answer.

"We could be waiting on that station now," Djako said, "that little island of a station back at the start of all this."

I thought about that island of a station and missed it. Missed who we were. Not because we were better or more innocent, but just because who we were, we'd never be again; never feel that moment just how we felt it then. But this proffered hope in this field now, because through the ebbing mist, we could feel something of significance as we'd never quite know this piece again and all its subtle shades.

The mist swirled on, and now dark trees loomed through the grey, giving great new horizons at barely few feet. So before us, we stepped into them, gaining new greatness through some simple softly-taken steps. And this simpleness was noted with a sigh of surrendered recognition, and relief to an extent.

How dark and cloistered these woods of silent firs were. How abandoned. And yet all was as it should be. What scent with no fault or suspicion we did know; it was pure and it was pine amongst elements of other fine things we needn't really know; like when making up tastes of cheese and wine when all you ever really wanted, and more so ever needed, was to consume and feel the marvel. What peace was here and some kind of weird wisdom that surely couldn't be for how could wisdom wander in a forgotten forest where no mind meddled?

The gate in the fence cracked behind us so that we lent ourselves a hope to fathom there might be someone there. But when we scrutinised through the dim, there was only unknown shape and shadow, no use to search and scrutiny. So the scrutiny was ceased and a pushing on resumed, and this reassured as our goal that awaited us was surely being approached.

Having pushed on a while further across this persisting plateau of ours, and then higher onto a rising peak, we took a short pause, breath rasping a little from the climb, and heads swirling a little from altitude maybe, or just something else like thinking.

"You know what," Djako gently panted with a nod over to one side, "I'm... gonna go round, there's a path here that forks off and it looks real nice."

"But we're practically at the top," I said, surprised at my pleading tone, "we must be nearly at the top..."

He laughed, shaking my hand and swinging on his rucksack, the hanging cups with no right to inside housing clinking in a comforting manner, even though that of the situation wasn't so.

"You'll... make it from here," he said, giving me one last look in the eyes as comforting clinking mixed confusingly with uncomforting sensations, "I'm gonna go round."

And then he whistled off along his path that seemed big, and discomfortingly clear, and welcoming.

I would push on alone then, undecided whether it be for better or for worse, or whether it made no difference either way. And mind was blown around by the wind that was picking up. And hands were laid cold by the cold that was coming down. But thoughts were looking up, to the top that loomed at last so close now. And even more saliently so, it seemed there stood a monument which grandly occupied this top, yes, some kind of church that must be marking the greatness of this place. And so climbing on and breath rasping to its limits now, I approached, and just like child's play after all, I saw I'd conquer this high place. And what but a triumphant smile could accompany my coming.

I scuffled in over the wall of the ruined old church, in the nick of time as this gale came down with all that it could muster, and there I'd shelter as the night came with it, and know a troubled sleep fraught with fever and half-consciousness, where deliriums of old days and memories that seethed, intertwined with the damp air that hung upon me.

And there it was, the time I collected shells on the beach with the one I loved, on a grey evening when no sun shone, or moon rose. When just waves rolled, and we were, and the wet evening air was. It was a grey evening, and we came to the beach where we'd been sometimes before. We didn't talk as we came; all seemed lost as we came; all seemed hopeless and in vain, and within was cold with confusion and then numb with nothingness, and then a falling hole. And then all these things again. We'd arrived and walked together, and ran together too, along the beach which stretched out along the edge of a silent town. Not a beautiful town; it seemed grey, and blocks towered to block out the view that could have been. Some people walked here and there, and they minded their own business, suffered their own trials, or relished their own happiness. And we walked past each other, indifferent, like we lived in other worlds.

Things were sad — I was sad — she was sad she couldn't make me not sad. So she'd try to make me smile but the beauty of her smile would only inspire tears. I walked ahead of her, and she followed on behind. I walked ahead so that in distancing myself from that which was beautiful in my life, the sadness and the hopelessness could be dampened just a little; if I could just keep walking and never look back, perhaps it could all be forgotten; including the poor duvet skills and how she'd failed to pack appropriately on our last trip together; and I could pretend to be at peace. But the sea arrived and I could walk no further and together again we came. So I looked away, at the water and the waves, and made light they too were beautiful, harboured peace and an- swer, or perhaps a thought for me. I would look at the sea, and not cry; listen and feel a while this salty spray and wet evening air that hung above me and clung to every heavy movement. But I'd come to feel alone and turn to see she'd walked away; she was walking away; I could see her big coat, red hat, and dark red flowing hair; yes, it was definitely her, walking away. I'd fumble down from the rock I'd stood upon, and stumble on towards her; hasten to her as I thought perhaps how she might not stop and never turn look back. But she would stop; she came to stop and turn look back to smile softly even then. And I looked back none the wiser, confusion swirling as relief rolled through to force out fear, yet anticipation with it too. So side by side we walked along by water's edge, wondering, sadness sapping still and throbbing on unremedied. And as we walked, I no- ticed a crunch, and another crunch, and then another, and though no mighty orchestra came to celebrate the crunch this time, this was no place or memory to stand something so slight, making silence through the wind and waves fittingly preferred as I looked down to see a thousand shells or maybe more there underfoot. And they were beautiful, shining out from the drab grey sand, like fallen jewels from a captain's chest, scattered to lie forgotten and know decay. As I pointed to one or two, she picked them up, the ones I'd chosen, and washed them in the sea. She was happy to collect these shells I chose, and I was happy to choose them for her. And as her hands grew full, and big coat pockets too, I smiled, and felt sadness slip away.

"...But they were just shells!" I came to find myself crying out aloud then in this dark little falling church upon the broken mountaintop, "...They were just SHELLS!"

And the stone walls of this church were smooth and wet and cold. And they blocked the view that could have been. And as I stumble through these broken corridors, I can feel the cold and rain sweeping down through worn-out roof above. And as this damp air is hanging on me, I can see her now, walking away, her dark red flowing hair.... And I cried and half-laughed and wondered if I'd ever know again, or if I'd known it well enough, that time, on the beach, on a grey evening, where no sun shone, with the one I loved.

I wandered the church as dawn broke, mulling my sleeping performance and composure in the night; it didn't seem as heroic as I'd have anticipated or liked, to mark my coming to the mountaintop. And meanwhile, shuffling around in old pockets and forgotten places, I fell upon the notebook

I'd seen Djako with as we'd stood by the station all that time ago and watched the little carriage that had brought us there trundle back the way we'd come. It was scuffed up and stuffed in a pocket. I opened it intrigued, to see all this that he'd been writing — his diary perhaps, poor jokes, or some failed love letters maybe. But it seemed all crossed and scribbled out, save for one line on a torn-off page which I found myself hearing aloud in his irritating voice.

"So let life bring me, and defeat me..." he said as I hummed sceptically and looked up in thought, while considering whether I was enjoying hearing his voice again or not, "...coz when my sky's bled all the light it had, no matter how I tried, death will come before me, and show me the kingdom I never knew."

I paused silent for I'm not sure how long and then wondered if I'd known him at all or just too well to notice; he can't have written this, apart from the use of low-quality conjunctions. These familiar words that rang surprisingly stark and close to heart without needing know their sense, that felt like they could have come from a soul I'd always thought was mine, or a brother I had once; they hung over me there on the floor of that church, and like the unreachability and unrealisableness of what they might mean to me or him, if anything at all, they blew away on the paper they were written, from my cold earthy shaking hands, and into the open arms of the roof above which was holey and gasping and waiting to get it all over with by a final falling in relief.

So the hour had come, in the nick of time, to throw down all arms, take leave of this forsaken place, and bid farewell this broken mountaintop. It was long ago forsaken, and maybe always was. *No...* it was forsaken the day man came and built his church, or temple, or whatever the hell this shit old building was; what a shoddy old botch job, like when Dad put up shelves one time. Because before that, the mountain stood wild and free, purpose far from even being conceived; it just boomed and breathed, and watched the trees, and grew them too with ease and free impression; what a goddamn artist. And maybe some wolves used to meet there to howl up at the moon, and we'd have awed from down below at their silhouettes all black and lone, harnessing such style before the silver glow. But then we just forsook it, through some kind of arrogance, or maybe just desperation, through the fires of dying consciousness, as hordes of wild conceited minds came burning through the broken line. It was all so damn classic. A chicken would have seen that coming from a mile away, and not even one of the good breeds — one of the stupid ones that doesn't lay eggs, or just eats them. So I'm taking leave of this forsaken place. I'm climbing back over this damn broken-down wall, and I'm murmuring how useless it all is, how mad it all is, how strange it all seems; yes I'm unfurling now, if not readily unravelling, as I stumble down away from this cold place. And I feel lighter already; I feel the breeze upon me come to gently push me on, encouraging me on, playing with this mangled hair. And I'm almost skipping now; I'm scuffing stones, scampering high, but being careful not to break brave bone or ankle lest one lose oneself along the way, as I look back, glance back with some sort of wry, and perhaps a grateful smile, or even one of disbelief; the mountaintop is fading now, falling back into the cloud, decaying on its own again, away all safe and sound. Though surging round the flanks, great bands of drizzle, rain, and hail, are blackening the sky; I can see them coming not far off, riding banks of thick dark fog I wouldn't doubt would will to lure and trick. But they're behind now, dropping back, far off this bold new pace that's come so fleetingly to foot; *they'll lash cold barren mountainside,* I softly uttered as I scampered, *finding no poor soul to hound and so booming on alone in hope of credence.* And I'm whistling now, or humming fair tunes, and thinking great things while murmuring already of how they're not so great. And it all seems so light, or comic, or rather completely inexplicable, with no mood to be explained. So I'm murmuring on as I push on, as the world is calling and great storms are stalling but rumbling onwards nonetheless. And I thought how perhaps I heard the toot of that train far down below; how I must be finding this train; but more importantly, how I must be getting home, before it become apparent that perseverance, and related things, might be pandered to or hallowed all in vain.

AUTHOR'S NOTE

I haven't included a formal dedication section, but here I'd pause to savour a thought for memories, childhood, family, and certain friends to an extent.

I should also note that just occasionally within the book, there are minor references alluding to certain people/characters that I don't necessarily know personally, but I feel have had a noticeable impact upon me through bringing some kind of lasting emotion or revelation to mind. I think I chose to include these references as a personal nod of recognition, and they might be called small dedications.

www.ingramcontent.com/pod-product-compliance
Ingram Content Group UK Ltd.
Pitfield, Milton Keynes, MK11 3LW, UK
UKHW040512041125
464644UK00012B/44